Dying to Live in
Palm Beach

Dear Marjorie and Michael—
How much fun has it been sharing our adventures since 1998—
Here's to lots, lots more ~
XOXO
Jane
3/2/13

Dying to Live in Palm Beach

JANE GROSSMAN

The characters and events portrayed in this book are fictitious. Any similarity to real persons, living or dead, is coincidental and not intended by the author.

Published by Thomas & Mercer
P.O. Box 400818
Las Vegas, NV 89140

ISBN-13: 9781612186924
ISBN-10: 1612186920

To my mother who encouraged me to write a story for Father's Day sixty years ago, and to my father who kept "The Mystery of the Missing Bagels" on his bookshelf for the rest of his life.

CAST OF CHARACTERS

The Girls (all are widows in their eighties):

Flossy Kane: A force of nature—willful yet wise. Once a beauty with great energy, she is recovering from a recent illness.

Bunny Boardman: Not a sparkling personality, but a ready companion.

Dottie Dornbush: Very social on the luncheon and benefit circuit. Donates generously to the most fashionable charities.

Betty Kantrowitz: Spiky and outspoken. Alternately puts people off and amuses them.

Mitzi Rosen: An incorrigible flirt. Multi-husbanded and looking for a new one.

Faith Spector: The most up-to-date on all the latest news and trends. Clear-headed and competent.

Gladys Spivack: Scatterbrained, but smarter than she usually acts.

Babs Tubman: The bridge organizer with a natural affinity for numbers.

~

Frances Cardozo: Flossy's Puerto Rican home-health-care aide. In her early fifties and long divorced.

Roberto Gonzales: Middle-aged detective with the Palm Beach Police Department. A confirmed bachelor.

Sy Zamore: Almost ninety. Has never married, although he likes the company of women and always has a steady.

Monsieur Michel Canard D'Argent: Chef of the eponymous restaurant the girls patronize on special occasions.

Additional characters include assorted other girlfriends and elderly men: Caroline, who is dying; Paula, who has Alzheimer's; Max, Sy's sidekick; Marty, in real estate; Sam Rabin, the new man in town…

CHAPTER ONE

Palm Beach is a high-gloss town. The blazing light bounces off the blue water, the white walls of the palatial villas at its edge, and the lacquer of the Bentleys in their driveways. It glints off the greens of the famous fairways and off the diamonds of the ladies in couture shopping on Worth Avenue.

— Judith Thurman in *Architectural Digest*, January 2008

It all started innocently enough.

She did not realize she had Bunny's credit card until she went shopping late that afternoon at The Flea. She popped in on her way home from the bridge game to see if she could find a new watchband. It wasn't that she needed a new watchband, not really; it was merely an excuse. She wandered up and down the aisles, playing an amusing little game with herself. Could she tell if the cheap merchandise that the flea market advertised as real designer goods was fake? Occasionally some items seemed genuine, but not legitimate—they were probably pirated off a truck on the way to the expensive boutiques on Worth Avenue. She often saw familiar faces from the society pages grabbing up these scarves and belts that had the most ostentatious logos. However, more often than not, she could discern that the Ralph Lauren logo was not quite the same polo player, or that the Gucci wallet was really a Cucci written with an elaborate C.

Besides, she had nothing to do that night. If she meandered around for an hour or so and picked up a few little things to cheer herself up, the lonely night would not seem as long. So she bought a new Cucci watchband and a snazzy pair of Ormani sunglasses, and spent only $19.00. She paid as always with her American Airlines credit card, as she accumulated frequent-flyer miles this way to occasionally fly back north for free. But as she tucked the card into her wallet, she noticed it was not her card.

It looked exactly like hers, but in fact, the name read Bunny Boardman. Flustered, she left quickly, deducing it would be pointless to go back and explain the mix-up to the elderly salesman with the two hearing aids. Yes, he was probably her age, but he seemed so doddering. She would call Bunny tomorrow and tell her their cards must have been mixed up at lunch before the bridge game, and she would give Bunny the $19.00 she charged.

But Bunny was not home the next day, and she never got around to calling, nor did Bunny call her.

CHAPTER TWO

"*Oy*," groaned Bunny as she lowered herself into her chair.

"*Oy g'vald*," seconded Flossy.

"*Veh iz mir!*" griped Dottie as she bent into the banquette.

"*Emmis*," groused Gladys.

"So I thought we weren't going to talk about our children today," quipped Faith as she joined the table greeting her seven friends, the regulars of the Tuesday bridge game.

Their routine was an old joke, but it never ceased to make them laugh. Their children were always a favorite topic of conversation, along with their physical aches and pains. It was only on rare occasions that they discussed the deep angst they felt, the fear and the loneliness that kept them up in the middle of the night. Mostly they kept it light, which is not to say they did not complain.

"So, Floss, where's Frances?"

"I persuaded her to drop me off for lunch, and I told her one of you would drive me to the game. She'll pick me up at four at your house, Bunny. Let me tell you, it is a relief to get rid of her. Nag, nag, nag. She makes me get up at an ungodly hour, then she subjects me to all these gadgets to test my respiration and heart and I don't know what. If she doesn't like the clothes I have chosen, she even tells me what to wear. Then pills, pills, pills…and the worst of all is she makes me eat breakfast. She is trying to get me fat so it looks like she's doing a good job. She's a pain in my rear! A nurse is no replacement for a husband."

"Humph," muttered Betty to Mitzi, she thought in a whisper. "Since when is Frances a nurse? She's an ordinary home-health-care aide, but Flossy thinks it makes her an aristocrat to have a *nurse*. So pretentious."

"No," denied Flossy. "As usual, Betty, you have it wrong. If you want to be an amateur psychologist, and amateur you are, here is why I call her a nurse: a nurse signifies that I am sick, and in my mind, Frances will stay with me until I get better; then she'll leave and I can be independent again. An aide signifies to me that I need her simply because I'm old, and I won't get better from that affliction, and she will stay forever. I have no intention of accepting the latter. And moreover, if you're wondering how I heard you with my deaf ears—that was easy. First, you are pretty deaf yourself so although you think you are whispering, you aren't, and second, I can *see* that you're talking about me by reading your lips. So, now that we have that settled, let's make up and have lunch."

Everyone else at the table looked on in silence as Betty blushed, but she got up and gave Flossy a hug and kiss and apologized. Flossy gave Betty a big hug and kiss right back and, for her, it was over. Unlike most of the girls, Flossy never held a grudge. Had the contretemps been between another two, they might not be talking again for weeks, but with Flossy, when it was over, it was over. The girls could not believe she was so easily forgiving, and of course, her little explanation touching on their most vulnerable subject made them all feel a little teary. But they got on with it…

"So how is Caroline?"

The sensitive subject of illness brought her immediately to all their minds. Caroline was dying, and everyone knew it. Up until recently she had rallied and joined them for lunch or a game, but not today. As brave as she was, her kidneys were failing, and she barely talked on the phone anymore. The question was pretty much directed to Flossy, who they knew called her every day. Most of the rest of them meant to but were just so busy that…

That what? Luckily the answer to that question was avoided as their favorite man, Sy Zamore, came over to the table. Sy was Dottie's "companion." He liked thinking of himself as the suave man about town, and in fact he was. Close to ninety, he was tall, still attractive, a debonair dresser, a passable bridge player, a good dancer, and a capable driver of a silver Mercedes convertible. Although he asked out the others from time to time, they only accepted when Dottie was away or her children were visiting. He considered himself unattached; they knew he was Dottie's.

Sy blew kisses to all and introduced his friend Sam Rabin, who was visiting from Boca Raton. All eyes were interested. He was hardly a prime specimen of manhood—not too much hair, a slight stature, and a turkey gullet, but hey, he had *driven himself* from Boca up to Palm Beach, and Sy said he was looking for an apartment in the area. There were few enough single men still alive, much less ones who could drive. It turns out he could play bridge too, as Sy was taking him to the duplicate that afternoon. Before any of the other girls could articulate an invitation, Mitzi jumped on it.

"Sy, why don't you bring Sam over this evening after the duplicate? The sunset from my terrace is just *gorgeous*, and I happen to know that the apartment next door to mine is going on the market, and it has the same delicious view. I'll open a bottle of wine and whip up a few hors d'oeuvres after our game and be ready for you and Sam around six," she drawled, putting on her best femme fatale. Mitzi always wore pink or lavender outfits with matching shoes and chiffon scarves. She batted her eyelashes and shook her blond curls just like the stereotypical southern girl she had been for over eighty years. But everyone who knew her well understood that underneath the sweetness was a crackerjack bridge player and a quick thinker who knew what she wanted and how to get it. So far she had gotten three husbands.

Sy began to demur, but Sam was already smitten, and he accepted on the spot. The girls all rolled their eyes, knowing Sam didn't have a chance, especially if Mitzi found out that Sam was rich as well as eligible.

Sy made his plans with Dottie for the night. This time she was taking him to the gala for the Association of Christians and Jews. He liked the fact that Dottie was so *branchée*, as they said in Paris. Palm Beach society had come a long way since he'd first migrated south in the winter, when the Christians and Jews never mixed at all. There were still some clubs that would not welcome him, but he and Dottie made a handsome couple; they were strategically philanthropic and got invited to most of *the* events of the season.

A few years ago when he was less emotionally attached to Dottie, he had had a real sneaker for Flossy, and he knew she had liked him too. Once, he even invited her to go to Italy with him, and he thought she was tempted, but in the end, she turned him down. He hoped Dottie did not notice that even now he had a soft spot for Floss. Most men did, but she and her late husband had been such an idealized couple, they worried they would not measure up.

And so the lunch was finished. The girls' favorite waiter took all eight credit cards and divided the bill—$16.84 each—and returned the cards to the table. While the girls debated the tip, the person who had Bunny's card made sure that this time she took her own from the pile.

She didn't say a word to Bunny, and clearly Bunny hadn't noticed she had the wrong card for almost five days. Once she had her own card back, it was too embarrassing to confess. She wondered if Bunny had used *her* card to charge anything, so she made a note to check her account online when she got home. It was the nineteenth, and the closing date of her bills was always the twentieth, so she could see if Bunny had used the card at all. What if Bunny had used *her* card for a big purchase? Should she call Citibank and deny the charge? Would Bunny notice the $19.00 charge at The Flea? This little folly was making her very anxious. Probably the best idea would be to bring it up at lunch the next week. She would innocently ask if anyone had been shopping where Bunny's charges were and then laughingly point out that they must have mistakenly exchanged cards at some point. She thought this would fly but was so distracted she made two really bad plays at bridge and lost $8.00 that afternoon—almost half of what she had spent with Bunny's card. How ridiculous she felt.

But when she checked online, Bunny had not used *her* card. She waited for several weeks, and when she knew Bunny must have paid her bill without noticing, she breathed a sigh of relief. That little game was definitely over.

CHAPTER THREE

"So did you hear the one about Mr. Schwartz and Mrs. Cohen?

"Mr. Schwartz and Mrs. Cohen live next door to each other. One day, Mr. Schwartz rings her doorbell. 'Mrs. Cohen,' he says, 'it has occurred to me that you and I each live in these big apartments, we each pay big utility bills and big maintenance bills and big tax bills. We could both save a lot of money if I moved in with you.' 'But Mr. Schwartz,' she replies, 'I only have one bedroom.' 'No problem,' he says, 'I will sleep on the sofa.'

"So Mr. Schwartz moves in with Mrs. Cohen and all goes well. In a week or so, he says, 'Mrs. Cohen, it is great living here with you, but my back is killing me from sleeping on your sofa. Couldn't I just come sleep in the giant king-size bed with you? You won't even know I am there.' 'I guess that would be okay,' she says, slightly nervous.

"So, Mr. Schwartz moves into the bedroom. A couple of days later, Mrs. Cohen has a complaint. 'Mr. Schwartz, I am having trouble sleeping. Every time I move, you keep poking me with your elbow!' 'Mrs. Cohen,' he replies, 'that's not my elbow…'

"'Mr. Schwartz,' she smiles, 'call me Selma…'"

There were lots of guffaws around the table. Betty was one of the few who ever told a dirty joke. It's not that they didn't enjoy them, it's just they were somewhat discomfited to tell them.

"So," queried Faith, "is this going to be the story of our Mitzi and the new man on the block, Sam Rabin? I heard she didn't play bridge on Tuesday because she was down visiting Sam in Boca, helping him decide which of his furniture would work in his new apartment. Fast work, I'd say. She just met him three weeks ago. And although he didn't buy in her building, I hear he bought a stunning apartment down the strip with views in every direction. That sounds like Mitzi's style."

"Well, I think it's great for her and probably greater for Sam," answered Flossy. "Let's face it, as much as we like each other, we all wish for a mate in our old age. I remember after Norman died, just a few weeks later I got a call from an old boyfriend who heard I was widowed. 'Do you still have the best figure on the beach?' he asked. What a line, huh? He hadn't seen me for sixty years, and all he wanted to do was come visit and, as he said, 'get to know me again.' He had become a Hollywood mogul, had been married three times, the last to the former Miss Greece, no less, and now he wanted me. Needless to say, I was flattered but, to say the least, *very* nervous. Once I got used to his old-man voice on the phone, I enjoyed talking to him, so I told him to come for the weekend. Luckily I still had some of Norman's Valium around, because here I was, eighty years old, feeling anxious as a sixteen-year-old on her first date."

"So—what happened? How come you are not living happily ever after?"

"So I'll tell you what happened...absolutely nothing. It was very disappointing. There was no chemistry between the pot-bellied old man from Beverly Hills wearing a gold chain on his sunken chest, and the wrinkled gray-haired lady who still had great legs. In any event, we spent the weekend together."

"*You spent the weekend together* so soon after Norman died!" blurted out Faith.

"Stop it. He stayed at a hotel. I'm not talking only about physical attraction; I'm talking about that je ne sais quoi, that certain feeling of wanting to *be* with a person. We talked on the phone after that once a week or so, and then he stopped calling. I heard he died..."

There was an unusual moment of silence—not for the death of the mogul from LA, but for their unspoken longing.

"All I am saying," explained Flossy, "is that Mitzi may be less discerning than I, but maybe I wish I were more like she is. I might be happier with a warm body in my bed, just to cuddle with."

"Me too."

"Me too."

"Forget discerning, I just wish someone would even *ask* me," mewled Gladys, who was not all that attractive. She broke the poignancy of the mood, and they all had a good laugh, and that was good.

"Hi, gang," greeted Mitzi as she blew in with a big smile on a cloud of Chanel No. 5. "What's so funny?"

"Nothing you would understand," sighed Gladys.

Mitzi looked at her quizzically, wondering if she should be insulted, but before she got the chance to process the comment, Flossy explained, "Mitzi, don't be upset. The girls are just jealous of your success with men." They all laughed again, mostly for the embarrassing truth.

Except for Betty. "Not *moi*," she exclaimed. "I am the merriest of widows. I'm thrilled to do whatever I want, whenever I want, on *my* schedule, wherever my whims and desires take me. Mitzi may get her kicks by flirting with men, but I get mine on my own."

"I think she doth protest too much."

Agreeing nods all around.

"Who wouldn't rather go to The Flea at night or play in one of my ninety-percent female bridge tournaments than go out to an elegant dinner at Canard D'Argent on the arm of an attentive man…even an old man?" asked Babs.

"Speaking of which," said Gladys, "there's a handsome devil for you!"

"Oh please, Gladys, Monsieur D'Argent is married, adores his wife, and is probably twenty years younger than you, anyway," said Babs, trying to dampen her ardor.

"But he always makes me feel so good when we go there. He makes me feel attractive and charming."

"Yes, and you keep going back whenever your family is in town, right? So don't you think he is just making sure he keeps your business?" asked Faith.

"You bet," agreed Gladys. "So if he makes me feel good, and I don't care why, I would very much like to invite you *all* there for my birthday next month!"

"We accept," they RSVP-ed in unison.

With lunch over, Babs the organizer and mathematician divided the bill, collected the credit cards, and gave them to their regular waiter, Jake. When he brought them back, they slipped from his hands, and one person picked them up and distributed them to their owners. But she exchanged hers for another's.

How could she do this again? For the thrill? Because it was so easy? Was life *so* boring that she would risk her reputation for a silly game? *But I have not done anything…yet*, she thought. *And I probably won't. I'll probably just hand it back next week…*

CHAPTER FOUR

It was a Wednesday, and Frances and Flossy were driving into town to do a little shopping. Frances was a steady, safe driver, but not quite fast or creative enough for Flossy. So Flossy tried to backseat drive, while Frances basically ignored her instructions by changing the subject. This morning they were discussing the upcoming birthday of Flossy's daughter when a car ran a red light and crossed in front of them. No one was hurt, as luckily Flossy was wearing her seat belt (a bone of contention between them), and Frances's quick reaction had braked their car in time.

"Mrs. Kane, aren't you glad I made you wear your seat belt?" exhaled Frances, a bit shaken.

"Oh, am I wearing it?" Flossy joked as she reached over to give Frances a hug as her way of saying *you did a great job.* "This reminds me of the old joke about the two ladies driving down Worth Avenue. One says to the other, 'You know, sweetie, if you keep running these lights, you are going to get a ticket!' 'Oh,' says the other, 'am I driving?' I guess it's more prophetic than funny. You know, I think I recognized the driver of that car…it was Paula Kramer, who, as I have been saying, is getting Alzheimer's. She should *not* be allowed to drive anymore...I am certainly a better driver than she is, and I'm not allowed to drive!"

Before Flossy could start to rant about not driving, Frances skillfully moved the conversation to where they should start their shopping. "How about Saks? If we buy something there, Zoë can always return it up north if it doesn't fit or if she doesn't like it. So what do you think if we start in the Armani department?"

The rant deflected, the two girlfriends proceeded to park and walk along Worth Avenue toward their destination. And girlfriends they were. Frances knew that Flossy called her "my nurse" with her group, but when they went out together, there was no hierarchy between them. Flossy had insisted she not wear her uniform on their jaunts, and in fact she out-labeled her employer when she got dressed up. With her Vuitton bag, Chanel flats, and Ann Klein pants suit, she looked as "Palm Beach" as Flossy, who, if anything, was less designer-labeled—which was not to say that the ladies at Chanel did not know her well, especially when the sales were on. The only hints of Frances's Puerto Rican verve (which she would never dissimulate) were her unnaturally red hair that she wore piled up on top of her head and the swing she added to her fifty-year-old sashay.

Flossy was as attractive as an eighty-something-year-old could be with her wavy salt-and-pepper hair cut in a casual bob and her always matching slacks, shirt, cardigan, bag, and shoes. She was recounting how she bought Zoë a new bag one year as she always saw her using the same black bag, day in and day out. She was so proud of buying something her daughter surely would need. But when she told her daughter why she had bought this gift, Zoë replied, "But Mom, you have given me tons of bags I never use—I can't be bothered changing my bag every day to match my clothes." Flossy changed her bags as routinely as she brushed her teeth and could not understand her daughter.

"Oh, Mrs. Kane," Frances consoled, counting on her fingers, "you brought up a girl who has a job, great kids, three grandbabies who adore her, a wonderful husband who needs her, dozens of friends, charities…no wonder she does not have time to change her bags." They linked arms in friendship (and for Flossy's stability) and agreed that Zoë was a good girl, even if she didn't care about style as much as they did.

As they entered the department store, they were greeted with warmth by the salesgirls in their favorite departments, joked with them about what was going on sale next, and got teased in turn about which cosmetics would make them young again. They finally decided on a luxurious black cashmere shawl for Zoë, which they both agreed she would use, since it would go with everything. While they waited for it to be wrapped, Flossy saw a friend from her bridge group out of the corner of her eye. She was standing at a counter across the floor. The salesgirl was handing her two large shopping bags and said, "Thank you, Mrs. Boardman." But it was not Bunny Boardman.

Perhaps she heard wrong or perhaps she was just thinking about Bunny, whose birthday would be coming up soon. At that moment Flossy's salesgirl brought out her charge card and asked her to sign the receipt. When she turned around, she saw the back of her friend disappearing down the escalator. How strange…

Flossy and Frances left soon after, and as always on their shopping expeditions, they had worked up an appetite for a "nice" lunch at Taboo, their favorite restaurant on Worth Avenue, where people went to see and be seen. They loved the action and loved to gossip about the players they knew for real or just knew from the "Shiny Sheet," the social page of the *Palm Beach Post*.

Even at midday, with the sun shining brilliantly outside, it was always kept very dark inside, and the atmosphere made Flossy and Frances feel very glamorous, knowing that only up close could anyone really tell they were quite senior citizens. It was not so long ago that Flossy was still given the eye by the posh denizens of the bar up front. Now Frances's big brown eyes attracted attention, but she demurely kept her focus on her patient.

Once they were settled at their table and served their aperitifs of Coca-Cola, Flossy told Frances of the strange sighting at Saks. Frances was skeptical. After all, Flossy did not hear that well, and she refused to wear her glasses unless positively necessary. Perhaps she *was* thinking of what to buy for Bunny, or perhaps she didn't really see who it was. "After all, if it was your friend, she surely would have come over to say hello, no?"

But Flossy was still unsettled, as much by what she *thought* she saw and heard as by Frances's explanation that she did not hear or see well. Should she ask her friend at the next bridge game in order to allay her own insecurities and find out if it really *was* her? There would probably be a reasonable explanation, and she would feel like a fool. And what if Frances was right that she couldn't hear and couldn't see? This was all ridiculous and painful speculation. She waved her hand back and forth across her eyes, as if to brush aside her thoughts and focus her mind. And when Flossy decided something, that was that! Most of the time.

CHAPTER FIVE

When she got home, she threw her shopping bags in the hall closet (she could not bear to look at what she had bought), poured herself a generous glass of Merlot, and walked out onto her terrace. She took ten deep breaths, a big gulp of wine, and stretched out on her chaise to think.

Pale blue sky and tall palm trees never failed to calm her nerves. Hers was a "side view" apartment, and she could see the ocean off to the east if she stood up, and that was enough for her. She did not need the full eastern exposure that some of her friends had; in fact, the full view of ocean and sky devoid of life made her feel insecure. It's why she didn't mind, she told herself, looking instead across the green lawn at the side of the apartment building next door. Seeing lights going on and off, occasional neighbors on their terraces, the cars driving into the parking lot, made her feel part of a community that was alive. The constant, empty blue of the sea sometimes looked too much like eternity, and she was unnerved by the image, knowing it was coming all too soon.

But in the meantime, what to do about more temporal problems?

She thought she'd had this latest escapade all figured out, but obviously she had not covered every contingency. Seeing Flossy and Frances at Saks was unexpected but should not have been. She could have bumped into any one of the girls while she was shopping and charging on Bunny's credit card. She just did not foresee that the salesgirl would say the name out loud as she returned the credit card—and not her own name, of course, but Bunny's. And she had panicked, running out of the store like a thief, for God's sake.

"Well," she said to herself as she sipped her wine, "I am a thief! The question is how do I become one who does not get caught? Am I smart enough to pull this off?"

She reviewed her new plan. She would go to the bridge group lunch, and while they were all taking out their cards after splitting the bill, she would distract them, and Bunny in particular, by announcing that she had received a call from the security department at Citibank. She would recount that they noticed an unusual amount of activity on her credit card, and they wanted to know if she had made purchases at Gucci and Ralph Lauren and Tiffany's to the tune of $8,816.75 that day. She thought not using a round number lent an air of veracity to the story. Absolutely *not*, she had told them, so the security department told her to tear up her card immediately and they would send her a new one. Furthermore, the nice young man on the phone told her that she should warn her friends, as there had been an abnormal amount of such credit card fraud in the Palm Beach area. They would all be clucking and sputtering with outrage and vowing to be careful as the waiter returned their cards. She would be sure to take her own this time, and Bunny would get hers.

She thought it was quite clever that *she* would be warning her friends about credit card fraud. Then, when Bunny did get her bill next month, she would not be shocked to see the $5,680.00 purchase at Saks but would immediately call Citibank customer service, deny making the purchases, and cancel her card. Phew! As she reviewed the scenario over and over in her mind, she sipped her wine, watched the sky darken, listened to the palm trees rustle, and started to relax.

But what about Flossy? Well, if Flossy had seen her, so what? There was not a reason in the world that she shouldn't be shopping at Saks. Obviously she would tell Flossy that she had not seen her, as she was so focused on rushing out to a hair appointment for which she was late. Totally logical. But! What if Flossy heard the saleslady call her Mrs. Boardman? Her heart fluttered a little at this possibility, but it was a long shot. First, Flossy was practically stone deaf, and with all the ambient noise in the store, she was highly unlikely to have heard anything. And furthermore, it would not take much to convince anyone that Flossy had heard wrong. She couldn't even hear bids these days unless they were shouted around the table.

She felt content and confident. So she went back inside to enjoy her purchases. When she had laid them all out on the bed, she relished the prospect of wearing the outfits she had "treated" herself to—one for night, one for day, and a smashing designer bag—the real thing. Now she just needed the right moment to wear them. Or maybe not. She tickled herself with the thought that she just might wear the day outfit to the bridge game.

The ringing phone interrupted her daydream, and she was reluctant to answer it, especially when she saw on her caller ID that it was Bunny. Why was Bunny calling right at this moment? Her made-up phone call from Citibank was so realistic; maybe it actually *happened* to Bunny today because of what she had bought at Saks on Bunny's card. And if that did happen, Bunny would have looked for the card in her bag and found hers and would naturally assume that she had used Bunny's to make all the purchases, and...and the game would be up! She would have to act shocked that she had been using Bunny's card and actually *pay* for what she had bought. Ridiculous, her sensible side said as she picked up the phone, but her heart was pounding out of her chest.

Bunny invited her to go out for a quick bite and a movie. She immediately accepted and breathed a long sigh of relief.

"Are you okay?" asked Bunny.

"Of course I am. Why do you ask?"

"I don't know, you just sounded so relieved to hear me ask you to go to the movies. And I know you're a movie buff, so…were you expecting bad news or something?"

"No, no," she laughed. "I was just running in from the terrace. It's such a beautiful evening, I'd love to go out."

And she thought she might even be able to switch credit cards back that night and not wait until Thursday. Then she promised herself not to fret over silly coincidences. Her confidence returned.

CHAPTER SIX

"So Sol's wife dies, and he gets all her life insurance. He had lived a sad little life and never spent much, especially as his wife was a miserable shrew. So now he takes the money, gets a face-lift, goes to Zegna and buys slick Italian suits, and buys himself a brand-new BMW convertible. He looks and feels like a million bucks, like a brand-new man. He's driving down Collins Avenue in Miami Beach with two gorgeous young babes in the car, and a bus hits him straight on; he dies immediately.

"Sol gets to heaven and beseeches God to tell him why he did that. 'God, God, how could you kill me like that, when, after years of suffering, I finally got to go out and have a good time?'

"God says, 'To tell you the truth, Sollie, I just didn't recognize you.'"

Pleased with herself, Gladys had just regaled the girls with a joke she heard from her brother up north.

"So do you think God still recognizes us, with all our fancy clothes and collagen?" queried Mitzi, who had had a lot more done to her face than collagen.

"I'll worry about that when I get there," answered Dottie. "I just need something new every time I go to one of those benefit dinners. Sy is so lucky. Men just get to wear the same tuxedo every time, but I *can't* wear the same dress. And do you know how much formal dresses cost these days? I can't afford it!"

"Puh-leez, Dot. Do you remember what everyone else wore the last time? Of course not. So why would they notice you? And besides, Dottie, dear, if you can afford to go to the balls at whatever they cost these days—five, ten thousand dollars—you can afford a few frocks," retorted Babs, who was always counting, whether it was their money or their cards.

"Me," moaned Gladys, "I am beginning to think if I wear new fancy clothes, someone *will* notice me. I mean, with some new fancy clothes, maybe some guy will think I am rich enough to marry, even if I am not gorgeous."

"Oh, Gladys, honey," consoled Mitzi. "Having had three husbands, and one in the offing, I can tell you that it's not what you wear, but what you do *not* wear that's important. I recently read a quotation from, I think, of all people, Robert De Niro: 'Women say they would rather undress in front of a man than a woman. Women are so judgmental, but men are merely grateful.' So a negligee and a good pocketbook are all you really need."

Titters all around.

"Well, what do we really need new clothes for anyway? I am of the opinion that it's just to make us feel good," said Faith, who was supported by Bunny.

"Clothes are for mood," stated Betty. "When I'm wearing something daring or spiffy, I feel ready for adventure. When I'm wearing old slacks and a golf shirt, I feel ready for the grave."

"Well, on that depressing note, let's do something fun. How about if we all join Sollie, ha ha, in Miami for a weekend?"

"Why would we want to go *there*? We don't belong in Miami," pooh-poohed Dottie.

"Dottie, you are an old snob," pointed out Bunny, although they all already knew it.

Gently Flossy put her hand on Dottie's arm and said, "Do you think we *belong* here? Do you think because you live on South

Ocean Boulevard and give your money to the right causes, you are *accepted* by Palm Beach society? When was your last invitation to the Everglades Club? Or Sy's? We have made our own lives here, and that's what community is…friends, family, and a way of life we enjoy. But let's not kid ourselves about where we *belong*."

As young women they had dreamed of Palm Beach, all its glamour and sophistication, so far from the immigrant lives of their parents. And their husbands had worked hard and made them very, very comfortable. Their dreams of Palm Beach came true, but they did not live in the Mizner-built mansions along the ocean, but rather in the very luxurious apartment buildings that had sprung up over the last twenty-five years just south of the mansion neighborhood. They belonged to country clubs—very lovely—but inland, in less desirable neighborhoods than the old, established clubs. Nevertheless, they shopped at the same stores for the same designer clothes, they drove the same luxury cars, and they flew first class… just not on their own planes. They were rich, but not very, very, very rich. They were educated, cultured, polite, and Jewish.

"But you are a snob too, Flossy," said Faith. "Think how you hate to go to that new club, Belle Rive, where all the nouveau riche belong, when we have a bridge tournament there."

"I don't deny it, but my snobbery is not based on religion or patrimony, it's based on behavior. For all my complaining about her, I would rather spend my time with Frances, who is a loving, caring person, than those creeps careening around in their Rolls-Royces. She is good company, she makes me laugh, and she does not try to hide that she came here twenty years ago from Puerto Rico."

"But Floss, you pay her to be your friend," sniped Betty.

Silence as Flossy's face reddened. She wondered what Betty had against Frances. Her friends wondered if she would be so fast to forgive Betty again. The silence continued as Flossy waited to choose the right words. "Betty, you could not *pay* to have a friend like Frances."

Everyone busied themselves with pulling out wallets and lipsticks, tissues to blow noses, cell phones to check calls from kids, anything to end this painful interchange. It was the right moment to change the subject.

She told the girls about her phone call from security at Citibank and how the unusual activity on her card raised a red flag in the computer system. She had certainly *not* done all the shopping that had shown up that day on her card, and the young man from security had told her she would not be responsible for it. But she was instructed to tear up her card immediately, and he would send her a new one right away. She showed them all her "new" card, for she had easily exchanged cards unbeknownst to Bunny at the movies the night before.

Warming up to her story, she warned, "The courteous young man told me that there has been a lot of credit card fraud in this neighborhood. And when I questioned him for details of where the victims had been shopping, he was pretty vague, but after prompting, he said mostly the department stores and lunch spots where it is easier to be anonymous than in the small boutiques. So I am telling you here and now to be careful with your cards! Look carefully at all the charges before paying your bills," she finished like a Cheshire cat.

At that moment their waiter pal Jake came to collect the credit cards. And now they looked at Jake in a new light. How easy it would be for Jake to take down a number, or even two, while he made up their individual bills. It's as if they all shared the same thought without ever saying it out loud. There was awkward coughing and hemming and shuffling about until Babs, their organizer, suggested, as if she had just thought of it, "Why don't we all pay cash? It's not a lot of money, and it's not worth the frequent-flyer miles we get for a few dollars, and it would make it so much easier for you, Jake, dear."

So each one gave Jake a twenty-dollar bill, and no one asked for change. Their twenty percent-plus tips were guilt money for suspecting Jake. They felt bad, but they were now wary of him, just a little. Even after their conversation about what belonging meant, it was still more comfortable to have qualms about someone who was not one of them.

For her, it could not have gone better. They bought her story, they suspected poor Jake, and she still had Bunny's credit card number. She really did not need the actual card anymore, especially if she was going to shop online.

CHAPTER SEVEN

"Mrs. Kane, why are you so blue this afternoon?" asked Frances as she picked her up from the card game. "Did you lose?"

"You usually read me like a book, Frances, but in fact I won eight dollars, and I'm more annoyed than blue."

"So tell your girlfriend Frances what happened."

"You know me, Frances—normally I would blurt it right out, but this time it has to do with you, and I…"

"*Ai, muchacha*, are you angry at *me*?"

"No, no, no, no, I am angry at Betty."

"HER! Now I think I am getting to the bottom of this. What did she say?"

"First tell me, Frances, why is she so resentful of you? Why does she take every opportunity to make some kind of a crack about you? This is the second time in as many weeks."

"You are so adorable, Mrs. Kane, worrying about me. Here is why she does not like me. You know that in my job my loyalty is to my patient, and if that means I have to be tough to someone else to protect my patient, or say what my patient will not say, I will do it.

"So you remember when I was working for Sandy Hirsch…"

"Of course I do. When I was in the hospital and knew I'd need help when I got out, I told Zoë, 'Find Frances!' I didn't even know your last name was Cardozo or where you lived, I just knew what great care you took of Sandy and how much she loved you."

"You knew it, because you called every day, just like you call Caroline, so she knows you're thinking about her. Your friend Betty used to call every day too, but with her it was questions, questions, questions. She had been a fine friend to Sandy when she was healthy, but she was like an inquisitor when Sandy got sick. She drove Sandy crazy, Flossy. Sandy was weak and dying and she didn't need Betty asking every detail of her symptoms and what the doctor said and then being all bossy and telling her what to do. Poor Sandy, she was so sweet—she would listen to this harangue every day and didn't know how to get off the phone. When Betty came to visit, it was even worse. So, as I said, you know what my job is. As Sandy got sicker and made it clear to me who she did and did not want to be with, I cut Betty off. I told her Sandy was too sick for visitors; I told her Sandy was in the bath or napping when she called. When she got around me and she did come, I would tell her to stop asking Sandy so many questions, because she was too weak to try and answer. So you see, I became the one who kept her from her friend in those last months, and she does not like me for it.

"Also, I would not be surprised if she resented that Sandy left me her clothes and a beautiful bracelet and only left her some costume jewelry. You know Betty always likes the *real* thing, and I gather she did not get much from her husband. So now that I have told you, what do you think?"

"Oh, Frances, I think you did absolutely the right thing, but I feel sorry for Betty too. She *tries* to be a good friend, but she has an unfortunate way about her that is sometimes abrasive. But she always includes me in everything she does. She is just missing some level of human compassion. She does the right things that a friend should do, but often doesn't do them well—there's a coldness there."

"I agree, Mrs. Kane. I am not angry with her, and I don't want *you* to be angry with her…I just don't like her. And promise me you won't let her drive you when she has had a few glasses of wine. Oh my God, that time she drove us to dinner I was reciting my Hail Marys all the way home!"

"Oh, Frances, you make me laugh. That's just one of the multitude of reasons why I like you so much. And your Hail Marys remind me of a joke my husband used to love to tell. It relates to the other conversation we were having at lunch about who does and does not belong in Palm Beach. Some of my friends are such snobs, and…oh well, here's the joke. It takes place in the nineteen forties when even the Breakers Hotel would not accept Jews.

"Abe walks into the Breakers and says, 'I'd like a rhoum, please.'

"'I am sorry sir, but we do not have any rooms available,' says the clerk.

"'Are you telling me den, dat you don't haf a rhoum for even von night?'

"'That's right, sir, not for tonight, tomorrow, or many nights to come.'

"'I don't belief you,' says Abe.

"'You see, sir, we do not accept guests of your type,' says the clerk.

"'And just vat is my type?' asks Abe.

"'Well, of the Jewish faith, sir.'

"'Me, Jewish, vat are you crazy? Ask me anyting, I'll show you I am not Jewish.'

"'Okay, sir,' says the clerk. 'Who is our Lord?'

"'Dat's easy, vhy Jesus, of course.'

"'And who was the mother of our Lord?'

"'Who don't know dat?' smiles Abe. 'It vas Mary.'

"'And who was Mary married to?'

"'These are sutch easy qvestions,' replies Abe. 'It vas Joseph.'

"'Only one more question then, sir. You have done very well,' says the clerk. 'Where did Mary and Joseph sleep the night that Jesus was born?'

"And Abe answers, 'Any imbecile knows the answer to this qvestion—IN A BARN, because a creep like you vouldn't let dem into the inn.'"

"Oh, Mrs. Kane," screamed Frances, "I don't know which makes me laugh more, the joke or your accent!" The tears streamed down her face as the two of them enjoyed the moment.

Meanwhile, down the strip, she was about to open her computer and start shopping at Neiman Marcus online…

CHAPTER EIGHT

"While others may argue about whether the world ends with a bang or a whimper, I just want to make sure mine doesn't end with a whine."

— Barbara Gordon, TV producer

The phone rang as she typed in Bunny's credit card number, and as she picked up the phone, she clicked "purchase." What a haul—five new nightgowns, a robe, four new pairs of golf shorts, two designer suits, and two evening dresses. She wished she could buy shoes online, but worried they would not fit, and how could she return them without the card itself? She had decided not to push her luck.

"Hello? Oh, hi, Bunny, you always call when I'm thinking of you. What's up?"

"Wait till you hear this!" exclaimed Bunny. "When I got home after the game, I told my bookkeeper your story, and…"

"Since when do you use a bookkeeper?" she tried to ask lightly to cover her anxiety. "You hardly ever buy anything."

"You're right, but last week when my son Roger was here, he was looking over my bills including my credit card statements, and he was asking me what all the charges were. To tell you the truth, I had no idea. It's hard enough for me to remember to pay my bills on time, much less remember what I spent where over a month ago! So I told him, I feel confident—although I didn't—that all those charges are mine as I never let my credit card out of my sight. I guess he was not too convinced because he insisted that I hire a bookkeeper to monitor and pay all my bills. Can you imagine? I acted insulted, but in truth, I am delighted not to have the responsibility.

"So, anyway, this is the second time I have had the bookkeeper over, and when I told her the fraud story you told at lunch, she downloaded or uploaded or whatever-loaded my credit card bill on the computer, and guess what! This is *so coincidental*. I had big charges at Saks I had *never* made, and the only reason I know it is because they were made the day my son was here, and we spent the whole day together. Can you imagine? The same thing happened to me as to you? Didn't you tell me you were shopping that day? You could have been there the exact same time as the person who stole *my* card? Do you think the thief looks like me?" Bunny rambled on and on.

She made sympathetic noises and tried to lower her pulse while Bunny told every detail of what had been purchased with her card. Of course she knew, as the items purchased were all hanging in her closet, so she did not have to pay too much attention. She had to think. This whole thing was getting too close for comfort. Bunny had made a good victim because she had never taken care of her own affairs—her husband had always done it, giving her whatever money she wanted whenever she wanted it. When he died, he left Bunny pretty incapable of managing anything except her life of bridge and golf. Now her son was taking over the role. What a nice boy, but how inconvenient. What to do?

She could cancel the online order—simple.

"What, Bunny?" She had missed Bunny's change of theme.

"Are you listening to me?"

"Of course I am. How lucky for you to have the bookkeeper, or you would have had to sort this all out yourself! Maybe I should get her name from you…I'm thinking I don't need the responsibility either—it would be great to have someone take charge of my finances." Well, not really; she was perfectly capable and always had been, but this would make Bunny feel better.

"Well, enough of this high finance," she joked. "Let's go to the movies tomorrow night. Whaddya say?"

Bunny agreed, and she offered to pick up Bunny at seven.

"But now what? Of course," she ruminated as she poured herself a glass of wine, "I will just go back online and cancel the order *tout de suite*!" She wandered out onto her terrace to watch the world turning gold in the sunset, and she thought how great she would look in the clothes she had bought. She thought how she would feel wearing them. She thought how much fun she had had buying them. She tried to imagine which outfit she would wear when they all went out to Canard D'Argent next month. She imagined looking beautiful.

But her skin was old, and her bones ached. Arthritis was creeping all over from her fingers to her toes. She remembered asking her doctor, after he had given her a clean bill of health, why, if she was so healthy, did everything hurt when she got out of bed in the morning. He had replied that it was because she was *old*. Well, she did not feel old. Her new "hobby" made her feel alive and young and attractive, not only from wearing her new things, but from how she had acquired them. "Maybe I am old in body, but my mind has never felt so electric," she pronounced to the world at large.

She went inside but did not cancel her online order. She thought about Bunny and how she was no longer a means to her pleasure but rather an impediment. The son and the bookkeeper were now looking over her shoulder. How to keep them from being suspicious? If Bunny were to die, they might wonder at $7,500 worth of clothing from Neiman's, but they would have no recourse. Bunny could not tell them anything. She would miss her companionship. Although none too bright, Bunny was a good egg. But there really was no choice. She was too happy in her new persona to let anyone get in her way.

She looked in her kitchen for fish oil, and not finding any, she ran out to the market. She bought the mildest she could find, something that did not smell too rank, but would still do the job. For Bunny was extremely allergic to fish, and she would go into anaphylactic shock from even the tiniest taste.

CHAPTER NINE

"Mrs. Kane, time to get up!"

"Oh, please, Frances, five more minutes! I am so tired."

"C'mon, Flossy-Flossy," she teased. "You have so much to do today, and first we have to test your heart rate and your respiration, and then we have to do your leg and arm exercises for strength, and then a shower and then weigh you and then…"

"*Stop*, Frances. That's why I need five more minutes. You tire me out before my day begins." She moaned, threw a pillow at Frances, and crawled underneath the covers and pretended to sleep.

"Meessus Ka-eene, I also have something to tell you that you will be very interested in." Silence. "Meessus Ka-eene, I have a *date* tonight!"

"With whom?" asked Flossy, suddenly wide-awake. She was keenly interested in Frances's social life, especially the lack thereof, and she was constantly trying to make a match. So far she had been unsuccessful, but not for lack of trying. She had proposed her widowed lawyer, her bachelor nephew, and her twice-divorced accountant. Frances had no interest in needy men.

"Hah, I knew I could get you up," said Frances, grinning. "I have a date with *you*. I decided since we have a boring day with the doctors today, we should go out to dinner and to the movies. Deal?"

"Deal," said Flossy, "but I still wish you would go out with my nephew, Lionel."

Frances crossed her eyes at the thought of going out with a fifty-five-year-old celibate named Lionel.

They got through the boring day of waiting rooms and check-ups and fairly good news from Flossy's doctors. They told her, "You're doing great!"

"Blah, blah, blah," muttered Flossy. She knew she would not drive again, nor would she play golf, and she would probably be dependent on Frances for the rest of her life. She sometimes felt like quitting, which was *not* who she liked to be. She knew she still liked some things about her life, but not as many as she used to, not too many at all. She missed her handsome husband.

Her children always told her how lucky she was, how most people her age would have died from the bout of lung disease she fought off last spring, how lucky she was not walking around with oxygen 24/7, how lucky she was to afford Frances, and Palm Beach, and on and on and on. They did not know what it felt like to be her age and losing her independence. She felt morose and peevish after these doctor days and knew how smart Frances was to plan a date.

And sure enough, a dinner at Canard D'Argent started to cheer Flossy. Monsieur D'Argent greeted them warmly and seated them prominently at the same table she had always reserved when her husband was alive. In most restaurants Flossy and her friends were resigned to being seated in the "widows' section" or "Siberia" after their husbands died, but here it was different. Monsieur D'Argent knew how they were treated at other establishments, so he went out of his way to continue to make them welcome. He knew it was good business to be popular with the widows, but he also sincerely cared about his customers, especially those he had known for so many years. He asked after Flossy's family. An amateur guitarist, he always remembered that her son shared the same passion, and he always asked when Zoë would be back down in Palm Beach, and when was he going to see those grown grandsons he had known since they were in short pants. But mostly he focused on Flossy. He told her how good she looked and how much he enjoyed seeing and talking to her. *The old flirt*, thought Flossy, but she thoroughly enjoyed being the object of his attention. And he did not leave out Frances either, knowing that making her comfortable too would continue to bring them back.

Then they were off to the movies.

And Bunny was there too with one of their other friends, but it was a big theater, and they didn't bump into one another walking in. Bunny and her friend, seated early, enjoyed munching on their popcorn and drinking their Cokes as the lights went down.

"Psst," whispered Bunny during the previews, "this popcorn tastes funny."

"Tastes delicious to me," she whispered back. "You probably have a bad taste in your mouth from the Thai spices at dinner. Wash it down with some more Coke."

Bunny gobbled down her popcorn, but a few minutes later she whispered again, "I feel kinda sick eating this. Will you take it back and ask for a new one?" Bunny's throat was starting to close.

"Of course, sweetheart," she replied. "I think you're right, maybe there *is* something wrong with the popcorn. I'll take mine back too. I'll be back in a sec."

It was a loud movie, and if Bunny gagged no one would hear her at all.

She ran up the aisle. She did not want to be there when it happened. She did not want to watch Bunny die. She was more upset than she had imagined when she planned this night down to the last detail. In fact, she was going to be sick. Running to the ladies' room, she barely made it inside before she vomited profusely. After shuddering on the cold tile floor, she wiped her face and prepared to confront the inevitable death of Bunny. In a cold sweat, she opened the door of the stall and walked right into Frances.

"Frances, what are you doing here?"

I am here with Mrs. Kane, and I just came to pee. I heard you being so sick. What can I do for you? What's wrong?"

"Oh, Frances, thank you so much for offering to help. I think Bunny and I ate some bad popcorn, or maybe it was something bad at dinner. I came to return the popcorn but never made it to the snack bar." She had spilled the popcorn all over the nasty wet bathroom floor and tried picking it up, but Frances did it for her and threw it all in the trash.

"You're right," said Frances, "It does have a peculiar smell, but maybe it's just this revolting bathroom. Let's go back and get Mrs. Boardman to drive you home."

"Okay," she replied shakily, "but you should get back to Flossy. And I will get Bunny to drive me home."

She knew she had been away from Bunny long enough. Bunny would be dead from the fish oil. The bottle was still in her pocketbook, which she clutched to her side, but she did not want to throw it away here in the theater, just in case. The suspicion would fall on the popcorn purveyor or the Thai restaurant where they had dinner. She walked slowly but purposefully down the aisle toward their seats, prepared to react.

"*Help, help*, somebody help!"

She screamed as she saw Bunny slumped down in her seat, her dead eyes agog, her mouth hanging open.

"Bunny, Bunny, Bunny," she cried as she tried to pick up her friend and hold her in her arms. Frances was there in a minute, as well as a doctor who was sitting nearby. They laid Bunny down in the aisle and took turns administering CPR, but to no avail. An ambulance arrived, but Bunny could not be revived.

Miraculously, she did not have to act. She was a mass of jelly, quivering and sobbing and being comforted by Frances and

Flossy. They offered to drive her home, but once she regained some composure she decided not to leave her car in the theater parking lot. She convinced Flossy and Frances that she could manage the short ride back home—she really wanted to be alone, so they followed her all the way to her building, just to make sure. She assured them she would take an Ambien and fall into bed. They promised to call her in the morning.

She did not take an Ambien and go to bed. Her body was vibrating with adrenalin. It had been horrible seeing Bunny's dead body, but now that it was done, she couldn't believe how well it had gone. She couldn't go to sleep, not yet. She had to prepare herself for the next few days, and she had to get rid of the fish oil bottle. Where better than the big wide ocean at her door? She slipped out of her apartment and went for a long walk on the beach. After a half mile or so, she tossed the bottle into the sea. She had never before walked on the beach at night, nor had she ever walked so far. But then again, she had never killed anyone before either. As she turned toward home, the wind began to gust, blowing the sand like hot needles into her face and legs. Leaning into the wind she slogged on. Overcome with an unbearable heaviness, she benchmarked her progress against the looming silhouettes of the apartment buildings, one after another after another, although in the darkness, they all looked pretty much alike. Dog-tired and emotionally drained, she really did not know what she was feeling. Earlier in the evening her body had made her vomit and cry, and yet she had been exhilarated. And now—now, she was frightened. "Please, God," she prayed, "don't leave me out here. Let me make it home, and I promise I won't do this again."

CHAPTER TEN

"I've had a perfectly wonderful evening, but this isn't it."
— Groucho Marx

Flossy and Frances were sitting at the breakfast table, talking about the events of last night. What a wonderful time they had had together until that terrible moment when they heard the scream in the movie theater. It seemed so surreal. One minute they were enjoying life, the next a friend had died.

They had gone over as much of the incident as they could piece together—Frances's experience in the ladies' room, the attempt to revive Bunny, the EMTs taking her away, the nice doctor trying to help and then console them, and the quiet, sad ride home following Flossy's friend who had been with Bunny for the evening.

"I've got to call her now and see how she is," declared Flossy. Just then the doorbell rang.

"Who is it?" called Frances as she walked to the door, prepared to authoritatively turn away anyone who showed up unannounced at eight thirty in the morning. Besides, she and Mrs. Kane were in their bathrobes, their faces completely unadorned—not in any state to greet anybody.

"Roberto Gonzales, from the Palm Beach Police Department, ma'am. I just need to ask you a few questions."

Frances hesitantly opened the door and found herself nose to nose with a very handsome man. Wiping her sleepy eyes, she stared at him in disbelief...not that he was a policeman, not that he had shown up at this hour in the morning, but that she was totally unprepared for the jolt to her psyche. She was interested in this man, and she had only known him for fifteen seconds. Flossy had told her about a book she was reading called *Blink*, in which people often made instinctive judgments, and the right ones, about people they hardly knew. And there was no way they could explain why they felt that way. So she stood transfixed as he smiled at her and asked, "May I come in?"

Frances regained her composure and, more sourly than she meant, snapped, "If you must, at this hour in the morning. You might have called first, you might have at least..."

"I'm so sorry, I didn't mean to offend you, but I must interview, as close to the incident as possible, everyone who was in the movie theater last night when your friend Mrs. Boardman died. I know you and Mrs. Kane were very upset and I knew it would be late to bother you at that hour of the night, especially in view of your loss, but I really must talk to you now." He smiled again, ruefully, and Frances was smitten.

"*Dios mio*," she muttered as she led him into the kitchen. *My prince has come and look what I look like—a mess, my hair a frizzy bird's nest, my face half asleep, my body hidden in this old terry robe—what chance will I ever have?*

"Mrs. Kane, let me present, um, Detective Roberto Gonzales. Is that right?"

"Yes, detective is right, but you can both relax and please call me Roberto." He addressed both of them, but he was looking right at Frances.

"But why do you have to interview us?" inquired Flossy as she observed the chemistry between Frances and Roberto.

"The police have been called in due to the unusual nature of Mrs. Boardman's death. Having already interviewed your friend down the road apiece, I feel quite certain already that her death resulted from an unfortunate set of circumstances, but I must complete my inquiry."

"What do you mean *unfortunate circumstances*?" demanded Flossy. She and Frances had presumed a heart attack.

"It appears that Mrs. Boardman died of anaphylactic shock, due to—the hospital has informed me this morning—the ingestion of fish oil. Apparently she was very, very allergic to fish. This might have come from her dinner, but as the allergic reaction is usually very swift, more likely it was from the popcorn she ate in the movie theater."

"I bet it was," piped up Frances, who until now had remained uncharacteristically mute. She recounted her meeting with their friend in the ladies' room, their friend's illness, and the peculiar unpleasant smell of the popcorn. "So will the popcorn seller be prosecuted for this? Wasn't it his fault?"

"It's not that clear," explained Roberto. "We'll test his popcorn machine, but he buys the corn from a large vendor, who buys it from the manufacturer, and you never know, some fish oil could have been mistakenly mixed with the corn oil somewhere along the line, and your friends could have been the unlucky ones to eat that batch."

"How awful for Bunny. She was always so careful, and I guess she never dreamed there could be anything fishy about popcorn. In fact, if something even smelled vaguely fishy, she would not go near it. How come she ate the popcorn, I wonder," mused Flossy. "And how awful to leave her there just for a few minutes and come back to find her dead. I must call my friend now, if you will excuse me."

"One moment more, Mrs. Kane, please. When you got to Mrs. Boardman's seat, did you notice anything you might want to tell me?"

"No, Roberto, just how ghastly Bunny looked and everyone screaming and crying. I can't imagine noticing anything outside of that."

"Thank you, Mrs. Kane. I'll just finish up with Frances, if I may."

"Frances, did you notice anything when you ran to Mrs. Boardman?"

"Noooo…only what I described to you in the bathroom. Will you try to find the popcorn I put in the garbage?"

"We will, but it will be next to impossible to find because it was picked up by the trash haulers at five this morning and taken to a dump southwest of here where they burn the trash twenty-four hours a day. But could you give me, perhaps, the blouse you were wearing last night? There could be traces of oil on it, and I'll bring it back to you tomorrow."

"Well, I doubt you'll find anything, as in my profession we are very careful when we touch things on dirty floors, and we wash our hands very thoroughly afterward. But I'm happy to give you my blouse anyway."

"Thanks, Frances." He smiled broadly as he left clutching her blouse. "And here is my card in case you think of anything else. Or even if you don't, just because maybe you would like to see me again?"

"I don't know that I'm the kind of girl to call a man," she teased, "but maybe I will be here tomorrow when you bring my blouse back."

"Say, at four o'clock?"

"Make it five, the funeral is at three."

"*Hasta luego, amiga.*"

CHAPTER ELEVEN

What a week! Not one, but two funerals.

First it was Bunny's, a full house. It seemed as if the whole country club attended along with the huge extended Boardman family and Detective Gonzales. Most did not know who he was, but she found it disconcerting to spot him there talking with Frances in the reception area. She knew her alibi was pretty foolproof, but it did not keep her from being wary. What did he have to do with Frances, anyway? She told herself she was being paranoid. After all, they were both Latinos and probably knew each other from some social club. Still, she would have to keep an eye on Frances.

The girls all gathered round her, clucking and cooing like a virtual henhouse of sympathizers, because she had been the last one to see Bunny alive. The family too was very solicitous. She was practically the belle of the ball…well, hardly a ball, but she rarely received this much attention, and she enjoyed it. As the irony of the situation came over her, she turned aside from everyone to shake it from her mind, and they all thought, of course, that she had just been overcome with grief. Could it have been more believable? Well, she was sad—sad she'd had to kill Bunny, but she didn't regret it, not at all. In fact, in honor of Bunny, she had worn her new suit, purchased at Neiman's.

It wasn't a tearful ceremony. The family was not an emotional one, more concerned with appearances than feelings. Bunny's husband, the scion of a self-made immigrant family, would have everyone believe his parents had arrived in America shortly after the Pilgrims. He had inherited a good deal of money and made even more on his own, thus enabling him to live the pretentious lifestyle to which he aspired. Sweet Bunny had no affectations and was just happy to be a part of his life. Their children seemed to follow in his footsteps. So there would be no fuss about how their mother had died—it was just a terrible accident. To discuss any other possibility would not have been respectable.

As for the girls, they sniffled quietly into their handkerchiefs, mourning for themselves as much as for Bunny. Flossy thought of her mother at these occasions. She remembered being the one who had to tell her mother—how old had she been at the time, eighty-two, eighty-three—that her beloved younger brother had died. She flew down to the modest hotel where her mother lived in Miami Beach, dreading the conversation. To her shock, her mother accepted the news with equanimity, shedding a few tears, but not falling apart as she had anticipated. "Thank God, my health is still okay," her mother had said. It was a revelation to Flossy, a revelation of the trench mentality by which old people lived. "I'm sad, but I am glad it's not me." And so they sat there, the hardened remaining few, having all experienced this too many times to enumerate. There should have been a prayer for them: "Dear God, take care of our friend Bunny, whom we will miss, but thank you, God, for not taking me."

They all filed out gratefully, glad to get outside into the bright, healthy sunlight, glad to be alive.

Two days later, they were back at the same place, nattering about everything and nothing, just to get the day over with. Their friend Caroline had died. Everyone knew it was coming, but twice in one week at the same funeral home was a bit much for their aging hearts.

It was a smaller group this time. Practically speaking, everyone had already said good-bye to Caroline months ago. Although they could barely acknowledge it to themselves, it had been too painful to call these last months. What could they say? What could they do to make her feel better? The rare times they did pick up the phone, they felt depressed all day, plagued by thoughts of Caroline's deterioration and fears of their own. So they postponed calling and said to themselves "the day just got away from me," or "I am so dog-tired," and put the call on their calendars for the next day or the next week. But Flossy called because she thought about how she would feel if she were lying at home day after day, afraid and alone, and the phone never rang. Her own illness had given her a preview, as the girls got on with their lives. So she took a deep breath and dialed every day. For two minutes she told Caroline a joke or complained about the weather. She hoped it helped; she knew she did it so she could live with herself.

The crowd was mostly female, except for the few men of their age left standing. Sy was there with Dottie. They were rather gaily dressed for a funeral, but they had just come from the annual St. Michael's Hospital breakfast at the Biltmore. Mitzi was dressed to seduce, as she knew her new young man would be there. (He was five years younger, but who was counting?) Faith, Flossy, and Babs were busy watching Max run his fingers through his wig as he approached Gladys. Gladys was working on her appearance, it seemed, as she was stylishly clad in a new Armani suit that, despite its svelte lines, did not make her look exactly thin.

"Uh-oh," pointed out Faith. "There goes Max, making his moves on Gladys. I wonder if she will stoop so low, just to get a guy, no pun intended. He's a persistent little fellow—I had the hardest time getting rid of him when he set his sights on me. After Irving, how could I even *look* at him? He sure is richer than Irving ever was, but he can't hold a candle in the brains or looks department."

"A man with delusions of adequacy," quipped Babs, quoting Walter Kerr, whom she claimed to have known in her youth from New York bridge circles. Whether she actually knew him or not, the quote was apt. They all looked at dull, homely Max and wondered why he was still alive and their husbands were not, particularly on a day like today.

Even Gladys, as anxious as she was to meet a fella, sloughed him off. Luckily she spotted Betty across the room and made her escape. Betty was full of beans and noted, "I saw you talking to the modest little man who has much to be modest about."

"I know you're quoting Churchill, as usual, and in this case it isn't even funny, it's just true," Gladys giggled. "Can you believe, I buy myself an Armani suit and a fancy designer bag, and *that's* what I attract? This is a sad day, oh of course it is. Caroline has died."

At that moment, they spied Marty, the real estate agent. "Ugh," groaned Betty. "There goes the *malech ha'moves* working the room. Look out, family!"

"*Malech ha*-whaat?" asked Faith.

"Come on, Faithie, I can't believe you, who knows *everything*, have never heard that expression," insisted Betty.

"It means, in Yiddish, Faith, dear, the one who takes the bodies away, but it is used to deride the people who hover around funerals waiting to benefit," explained Babs.

"I really never heard that expression, honestly," said Faith, ironically crossing her heart.

"Me neither," added Flossy, "but it certainly is onomatopoeic. I may not be able to hear that well, but it sounds like a ghost to me, mooooo-vissss."

They all laughed, but out of respect for Caroline, not too loudly. "So what's so funny, girls?" asked Marty as he strolled over to greet them.

This time they erupted in peals of laughter, despite the inappropriateness of the occasion, and felt like teenagers. Each time they caught each other's eyes, they guffawed again.

"Really, ladies, this is such a sad occasion, how can you laugh? I mean, it's not as sad as Bunny's death, which was so shocking. By the way, the Boardman family has asked me to sell Bunny's apartment."

"We're not really surprised," snorted Betty, while the rest of the girls tried to control themselves.

"Of course not," preened Marty. "I am an old, old friend of the family. By the way, have you seen Caroline's son? I need to talk to him. You know, I mean pay my respects."

"I believe he is in the sanctuary, Marty," replied Flossy. "You might give him a little peace."

"Of course, of course," nodded Marty as he strolled off to network some more, never knowing who would die next but feeling sure he would have plenty of future customers represented in the room.

CHAPTER TWELVE

"So is it possible that chicken soup gives you a cold?"
— Nora Ephron

"Did you read the absolutely hysterical op-ed by Nora Ephron reprinted in the *Times* the other day?" asked Mitzi. She had joined the girls for lunch after Caroline's funeral, as her latest Mr. Right did not show up. "A bit of reflux, he complained." She hoped he wasn't having a heart attack.

"I think Nora was right. Google will be the end of conversation. All my kids and grandkids do is sit in front of their computers looking for the answers to everything in life, from what time the movie starts to why the baby is coughing, to…I don't know, explicating the theories of Stephen Hawking," pronounced Babs. "My kids want me to play bridge online, but I keep telling them, 'over my dead body.' I will play bridge online when I *can't* go out anymore, but not before. They don't understand that playing bridge gets me out into the world meeting real, breathing people. Why would I want to stay home and play alone?"

"The lonely times are long enough," empathized Faith on the same wavelength.

"I agree," chimed in Dottie, who had joined the girls too. Sy had gone off to play nine holes, which he always did after a funeral, just to prove that he could. "Picture this—Sy says in a thousand years humans will have gigantic bulging eyes, long, powerful fingers and wrists, skinny arms and legs, and fat bottoms, because all their lives will take place on the web. They will even have sex online!"

"I wonder if we could do that now?" tittered Gladys. "I mean, it would be better than nothing, and it's something new. Probably beats sleeping with these old guys we have hanging around us."

"Hey, don't disparage my fella," protested Dottie. "He's a good, um, ah, snuggler."

"Hey, sweetheart, don't give up yet. I certainly haven't," proclaimed Betty. They all knew that she talked a good game, but she had a better imagination than love life.

"Me too," said Mitzi. "I am still in the game...well, as long as the lights are out." And they knew that she was.

"Me too!" piped up Paula, who had joined the girls for lunch. "I think that Dr. Ephron was right too. Breast-feeding does cause allergies."

Flossy had kindly invited her to come along, knowing how really alone Paula was. As her mind deteriorated, she got fewer and fewer invitations to play bridge or even to go out to the movies. Remembering the near-miss car accident with Paula, Flossy had offered to pick her up with Frances and bring her back home. She was lucid at the time and very grateful. But now she had lost track of the conversation.

"I read that article by Dr. Ephron in the *Times*, and she proved, quite logically, that because all the young mothers are breast-feeding now, and more and more children have allergies to peanut butter and fish and things, it must be from breast milk."

"*Pau-lah*," cackled Betty, "Nora Ephron was not a *doctor*, she was a humor writer. It was a *joke*."

No one else laughed, as they saw the devastated expression on Paula's face. Flossy's eyes sent daggers across the table at Betty. She could handle Betty's nasty side, but poor Paula could not.

"But Faith, your husband was a doctor, don't you agree with me?" pleaded Paula, more muddled than ever.

"I understand what you are saying, Paula, sweet. We all do. It does make sense. Don't you worry about silly Betty," Faith comforted as she put her arm around her from one side and Flossy embraced her on the other.

At that moment, they all heard a buzzing sound coming from Paula's handbag. Paula did not seem to notice. But even Flossy could hear it.

"There is something buzzing in your pocketbook, Paula. Do you know what it is?"

"Oh, yes, yes," she beamed, having totally forgotten her little run-in with Betty. "My daughters have given me a special pocket alarm set for the hours I am supposed to take my pills. See, I have them all arranged in this container, and I take them four times a day."

She held out the little pink pill dispenser for all to see. There were four little pockets in the container, each containing four pills, each clearly labeled nine a.m., one p.m., five p.m., and ten p.m. "I have one for each day of the week, and they are all different colors, and I know this is Friday, because Friday is pink. The pill nurse fills them up for me every Monday when she visits." With that, she turned off her alarm and popped the pills into her mouth. "Isn't this clever? I take different pills at different times of the day, and this way I never mix them up and always take them on time," she announced.

"And I don't have to have someone bothering me to take my pills every day, like you do, Flossy, dear."

"Well, no good deed goes unpunished," murmured Flossy, knowing that Paula meant no harm, but she did not enjoy being reminded by someone who had only half a brain that she was dependent on Frances.

Out loud she said, "You know, Paula, dearest, I understand your desire to stay independent, but it certainly is a pleasure to have someone else do the driving. Don't you think it would be good to have someone like Frances drive you?"

"Oh, absolutely not…I am a *very* safe driver."

"Uh, and you almost killed us on Worth Avenue last week," is what she wanted to retort, but instead said gently, "Well, I guess we all have to pay more attention to what we're doing these days."

"Speaking of Frances, Floss, tell us about the handsome man Frances is lunching with across the room!"

"Ohhhh, that cute guy is her new, dare I say, romance. He's Detective Gonzales, and he was investigating Bunny's death. He came to interview Frances and me because we were at the movies that night too. It was just a pro forma visit, but I don't think he would have paid me a bit of attention had I seen a six-foot-ten gorilla carrying a high-powered rifle. From the minute he walked in the door, he only had eyes for Frances. She says they are just friends, but I think otherwise. I could feel the chemistry in the room. I mean I don't think she is sleeping with him… yet. They only meet for a couple of hours during the day when I have something to do—you know, like the hairdresser or bridge, whatever."

"Well, wouldn't that be nice for Frances," they all assented, dreaming of their earlier days when they were struck by the chemistry of love, or just plain sex.

With a deep group sigh, they paid their bill and got ready to leave. Since the credit card fraud story, they still eyed their waiter, Jake, with a bit of anxiety, and they paid cash. Flossy looked at her watch, and realizing she would be late for her manicure, she waved to Frances that they had to get going. "Can anyone give Paula a ride back home? Frances and I have to scoot."

"Sure, I will," she replied. "We live in the same building." She had nothing better to do that afternoon besides going to The Flea. And she had an idea percolating. Maybe she should take Paula with her to The Flea, and they could buy a few things together. It was coming together in her head faster than she could believe.

CHAPTER THIRTEEN

"I remember now! Dr. Ephron wrote that book about hating her neck and other things about getting old, right?"

"That's exactly right, Paula, dear. She did write that book. Did you read it?"

"I did, and I just don't believe her on *everything*."

"Because?"

"Because she said she spent ten thousand dollars on fixing her teeth and thousands more on Botox and I don't know what else. Do you think she really did, or is she just trying to make sure you know how rich she is? I mean, who would spend all that money on their choppers?" She giggled at her own turn of phrase.

"Oh, Paula, maybe it was a slight exaggeration to make a point, but the idea was about feeling insecure at a certain age, and we all can identify with that because..."

Before she could finish, Paula was off meandering about something else. She did not have to answer, as Paula was just happy to have company to listen to her ramblings.

"And so I said to her I will never take rat poison to get rid of wrinkles..."

"Paula, you said what to whom?" Why did she bother? Paula's senility had no logic, but she was not totally out of it. That had been a shrewd comment she made about Flossy needing Frances all the time. Like many senile people she knew, Paula sometimes had moments of intuition. She had better not let down her guard.

"So, Paula, would you like to go to The Flea with me before I take you home?"

"I would love to. I can never remember how to get there, and I need so many things. I always used to buy a watch there every week, but they don't have tomatoes, do they?"

She sighed and gave Paula a big phony smile as she slipped into the parking lot at The Flea. Paula was off and running. After an hour, Paula was laden down with myriad tchotchkes, faux designer sunglasses, and watches, and she needed help to pay.

It was just as she had foreseen. "Let me help you, Paula. Give me your wallet, and I'll get out your credit card for you." Which she did, but she also slipped Paula's American Express card into her pocket while handing Paula her MasterCard.

Back at Paula's apartment, they had a cup of tea together on the terrace and watched the sun set, and when Paula's alarm went off again, they went into the kitchen together. Paula's pill dispensers were lined up in chronological order on the counter, taking up most of the space, so as she slid the tea service onto the counter beside them, she knocked all the dispensers to the floor. There were pills everywhere. She jumped back in mock horror at the mess she had created.

"Oh dear, are you okay?" asked Paula plaintively as she stared at the riot of pills all over her kitchen.

"Of course I am, Paula, dear," she replied, feeling so pleased with her effortless sleight of hand. "But what are we going to do about all this confusion of pills? Do you know which ones you take when?"

"No…no, I don't," whimpered Paula. "I guess I could call the pill nurse to come over tomorrow, but I put today's dispenser right here in the line too, so what will I do about right now and then tonight before bed?"

"Don't be upset, Paula, sweet. Do you have the bottles here?"

"Yes, I do, but they put them on a high shelf where I can't reach them and take them by accident, like I did the time I took the sleeping pills in the morning and the happy pills at night and got so messed up. Oh, oh, what can we do?"

This was perfect. She didn't know that Paula had reversed her pills, but she'd heard that she had been sleeping all day long. No wonder Paula's daughters had come down and hired a visiting nurse to manage their mother's medications. "Show me where they are, dear."

"Way, way up above the refrigerator. They think I don't know, but I'm more observant than people think!" Paula replied with a smile of self-satisfaction.

As she climbed up on a step stool to retrieve Paula's prescription bottles, she exclaimed, "I have a brilliant idea! Let's call Frances and ask her to come over and put all the pills back in order for you. She's very experienced with all these drugs, and I know she can help us!"

"Oh yes, yes, I'll call right now." And Paula jumped up and down clapping her hands like a child.

Frances was happy to help. She arrived in ten minutes, and although she had reservations about the responsibility, she recognized all the pills Paula was taking, and she quickly and efficiently put them back where they belonged in their little pastel dispensers. She then climbed back up to the cabinet and secured the bottles out of Paula's reach. "I'm happy to help, ladies, but I'm outta here…Flossy and I are going out to dinner and I have to change. *Adios*!" She waved as she dashed out the door.

"My, my, it *is* almost dinner time, Paula. Do you have food for dinner?" she asked as she peered into Paula's refrigerator. There wasn't much besides a very little chicken pie and a very large pecan pie.

"I have just what I need for tonight," Paula announced as she stuck her head into the refrigerator. "I have a little main course and a nice big sweet dessert. You know, I eat the dessert first, and then I have the main course if I am still hungry." She smiled, pleased with her naughtiness. "I got the idea from my son-in-law years ago. We used to go to the country club all together on buffet night, and he always headed right to the dessert table first. He ate two or three portions of cake at least, and then he had roast beef for dessert! I thought it was a terrible idea then, but now I have seen the light. It's so much more nutritious!"

"Well, Paula, sweet, I hope you are taking your vitamins too. It does not seem so healthy to me."

"Vitamins, schmitamins, I am as healthy as a house."

"I think you mean healthy as a horse, Paula, but I get the idea, and you are in good shape, as long as you take your pills on time and correctly. So don't forget to take them now, and then again before bed. And I'll tell you what—I have an enormous carrot cake at home that my grandchildren sent me. I will never be able to eat it all. How about if I bring it over to you tomorrow evening for your dinner? Is there anything else you need, darling?"

"Oh, I just adore carrot cake, and it's so vegetarian," cooed Paula. "I especially love icing. If I have any room afterward I can always open a can of tuna."

"I doubt you will," she said under her breath as she gathered up her things. She deftly reordered the pills Frances had arranged in the Friday and Saturday dispensers. "Toodle-oo...and don't forget to take your pills! I'll be back tomorrow."

She watched Paula swallow down her pills as she left.

CHAPTER FOURTEEN

"Life is always acting."

— Lupita Tovar, ninety-seven-year-old Mexican film star

She turned on the radio, and while listening to an interview with a venerated old actress who had appeared in the first Mexican talkie, she fairly danced around the apartment. This was going to be so easy. She was a natural, and she had had no idea in all her eighty-three years that she could be so cleverly devious. Until two weeks ago, she had always accepted her wearisome fate: a typical suburban life, comfortable, to be sure, but with no spark, no thrills, no *risks*! She had borne and accepted it for so many unexciting years.

Lupita, the Mexican actress, went on to reflect, "Sometimes, you know, I am here at home at night, and I start thinking back, 'Would I change anything?' No, I will do exactly as I did."

"Well, not *me*," she shouted. "I would have changed a lot, but I didn't for all those years, and now...now, finally, I am! I am learning to be an actress at the ripe old age of eighty-three. Although maybe *this* is the real me, and I was always acting before." The difficulty of wrestling with the evolution of her new self was too disconcerting. "Besides," she interrupted herself as she poured a glass of Chardonnay, "it's time to get down to details."

She had palmed the strong sleeping pills, Restoril, she had found stashed way in the back of Paula's cabinet, not the mild Ambien that went into her pill dispensers. She crushed them to a powder and mixed them with the half dozen Xanax she had stolen as well. Having reversed the order of Paula's pills for tonight and tomorrow, she had ensured that Paula's already addled brain would be further confused—she would be up all night and groggy all day. So when she returned tomorrow evening with the drug-laced carrot cake, Paula would never notice a slight bitterness under the cloying sweetness of the icing.

"What a stroke of sheer brilliance to get Frances over there, if I do say so myself!" Frances was always showing up—first at Saks, then at the movie theater. Pure coincidence, of course, but now *she* had initiated Frances's proximity to the crime. Not only would this ploy undergird her own innocence, but also it just might throw a bit of suspicion, should there be any suspicion at all, on Frances. She had seen how the girls were all eager to blame Jake, their waiter, for stealing credit cards. If necessary, how easy it would be to cast aspersions on the other outsider in their lives, the Puerto Rican.

And as for her shopping day tomorrow, it could not be online. She took that chance once with Bunny's card, but clearly no one was following up on the purchases Bunny had allegedly made in the few days before she died that got delivered to *her*. No, this time she would go shopping in person, but not for clothes and not on Worth Avenue. Too many new clothes would certainly raise eyebrows among her friends, so it would have to be things she coveted that no one but she would appreciate. She would go out to the malls in West Palm Beach and buy all new Pratesi sheets and towels at Pioneer Linen and gorgeous lacy underthings at La Perla. She giggled at the thought of a black lace thong on her drooping rear end and a push-up bra doing yeoman's work on breasts that had long ago succumbed to gravity.

And as she made her tuna fish sandwich, she thought she might stop at that new delicacy store and buy some beluga, not plebian old osetra, and a bit of foie gras, and...something else, an impulse purchase for no reason at all, except that she could.

She thought of the punch line to the joke about Sol—that God had knocked him off because he did not recognize the new Sol. She hoped He would still recognize her. She put down her glass, and with a clong in her heart, she realized He would not. She was a murderer now. Well, it was too late to obviate that sin, and she had been so good for so long, and for what reward? She drained her glass, mopped up the crumbs of tuna fish, and thought of the joke where every night God serves a tuna fish sandwich to Moses. Meanwhile, down below in hell, Moses sees everyone eating huge steaks, briskets, pheasants, pastries, truffles, and champagne. Sick of tuna every night, Moses meekly (yup, just like her) asks how come, after such an obedient and pious life, he gets tuna, and in hell they eat like kings. God replies, "For just two people, does it pay to cook?" There probably were only two people in heaven. She sure did not want tuna for eternity, and everyone else seemed to be having a better time. Enjoying her metaphor, she rationalized herself to sleep. She had already forgotten her vow to God that she would never murder again.

The next morning she followed her plan and scooted out to the malls first thing. Loaded down with packages, she hustled through the parking lot and bumped right into Frances and Flossy. Shocked, she blurted out, "What are you doing here?"

"Well, I guess by the look of you, not doing quite as much shopping as you are," Flossy replied curtly.

"I'm so sorry, I didn't mean to sound so abrupt, it's just I am running around getting ready for my kids to come down next month. I had ordered new bed linens, and they came in wrong and I was so annoyed I just bought any old replacements, and now I have a thousand things to do today, and this has put me behind the eight ball, and...phew! I know none of this is important; I am just getting a bit *farmisht.* I should stop and breathe and have a cup of tea with you, but I've gotta run."

"No problem," said Flossy as she smiled with understanding. "I know how it feels to have the children invade. I adore my kids and grandchildren, but there's always so much chaos when they come down. Let's face it, we're getting used to our uncomplicated way of life, and we feel unsettled when we get disrupted—even for a good reason, like the kids. So don't worry about us; we understand completely."

"By the way," asked Frances, "did you talk to Paula this morning? She seemed so upset when I left yesterday, we decided to call her, but there was no answer."

"No, I left so early this morning, and I thought she would sleep late, so I didn't want to wake her. I'll call later. But trust me, she was fine last night, looking forward to her pecan pie for dinner. Do you know she told me she eats her dessert first and then, if she has room, eats her main course?"

"Sounds like the diet I would follow, if Frances would let me!" teased Flossy as she wrapped her arm around Frances's and strolled off.

As she drove home, she breathed a sigh of relief, wondering why she had to bump into them yet again. Luckily they had not seen her buying caviar and pâté de foie gras and the exquisitely tooled little tortoise-shell spoon and spreader to go with them. How would she have made up a quick story about that? Hopefully they had not noticed the Pratesi labels on her sheets…

The day crawled by, and she did not lose her nerve, but she was in high adrenalin mode. She remade her bed with her elegant new linens, took a long bath, and luxuriated in her new towels, trying to keep calm. By late afternoon, she decided it was time.

She walked up the stairs to Paula's apartment carrying two huge portions of carrot cake. No sense letting anyone see her in the elevator to pinpoint her whereabouts. One portion she would leave in the refrigerator; the other, already adulterated with Xanax and sleeping pills, she would give to Paula for tonight's dinner. Paula's Amex card was tucked in her pocket.

Paula greeted her and hungrily eyed the carrot cake while she complained of feeling logy and headachy all day. "Must've been the blackbirds baked in my pie," Paula chirped.

"Or more likely too much cake and not enough real food. Let me get you an aspirin and see if I can help you set up for dinner," she offered as she marched off into the bathroom. On the way, she slipped Paula's Amex card onto the desk next to her pocketbook, carefully wiping it with tissue so it would be free of her fingerprints.

In the bathroom, she hit the jackpot. Not only did she find aspirin, but also an almost full bottle of oxycodone prescribed by Paula's dentist. He must have given it to Paula for pain when she had her implants done last year. Well, they would still be potent enough to add the final touch to her baking. She knocked over the bottle and scooped up the pills. Wiping around carefully, she returned to Paula carrying the aspirin and empty oxycodone bottle.

"Paula, dearest, what is this I found in your medicine chest?" she asked, handing her the bottle.

Perusing the prescription, Paula answered, "Oh, this is oxygen from my dentist, and I don't need it anymore." Paula tossed the bottle in the wastebasket and, swallowing her aspirin, hovered over the cake. "Can I eat it now?"

"Wait, sweetie," she replied, "it's been in the refrigerator, and it should warm up a bit so you can get the full flavor. Why don't you go lie down on the terrace and I'll bring you a cup of tea and your pills. Didn't I hear the alarm go off when I was in the bathroom?"

"Yes, yes, you did, and I was just about to take them. Thank you so much." And Paula drifted off.

She took the opportunity to crush a half dozen of the oxycodone into the cake and drop the remaining powder into the tea. With a huge dollop of honey in the cup, Paula would never notice.

She had been slightly anxious that the combination of Xanax and sleeping pills would not have been enough to put Paula to sleep forever, but now she felt certain she had mixed more than enough drugs with deadly interaction. Just like poor Heath Ledger…Paula would like the idea of dying like a movie star.

After Paula finished her tea, she took the cups and saucers, rinsed them, and turned on the dishwasher. Using her tissues for gloves, she laid out some cold cuts she found in the refrigerator and the huge piece of laced cake. Wiping everything around with a dishcloth she stuck in her shirt, she kissed Paula good-bye and told her that dinner was ready whenever she was, but she should really wait another hour or so for the cake to blossom into its full, sweet flavor.

She quietly dashed down the stairs and made one more move. Knowing Paula would still be on the terrace, she called and left a message, "Paula, dear, as you are not answering the phone, I left a huge piece of carrot cake at your front door—enough for at least two nights. Enjoy!"

CHAPTER FIFTEEN

"So Harry is sitting at the Super Bowl and notices that there is an empty seat next to the man across the aisle. He asks the man, 'Does that seat belong to you?'

"'Yes,' the man replies mournfully. 'It is the seat of my beloved wife who passed away. We attended every Super Bowl together for many, many years—and it is empty in her honor.'

"'But it's a crime to waste a Super Bowl seat,' says Harry. 'Couldn't you invite someone else—a family member, a friend, a colleague from the office?'

"'Unfortunately no…they're all at the funeral.'"

The men all roared, wiping the tears from their eyes. It was a rainy Sunday, so no golf. They were lingering at their usual table at the country club, finishing up brunch. Sy chuckled. "That reminds me of the one about the old guy who is about to marry his fourth wife. Each time they get younger and younger and this babe is especially sexy."

"We know it, Sy, we know it."

Undeterred, Sy carried on. It didn't matter because they all repeated themselves, and they were tolerant of each other. Besides, they loved this joke.

"So they go to the doc for their pre-marital checkups. The doc walks into the examining room and says to the old guy, 'Now listen, I know you are going on a beautiful honeymoon to a romantic beach resort, but I want you to take it easy. You know that too much sex can cause a heart attack or even a stroke.'

"And the old guy replies with a shrug of his shoulders, 'So if she dies, she dies.'"

At that moment Betty walked by the table on her way to join the girls. Overhearing their conversation, she poked her head between Sy and Marty and whispered, "You wish, guys, you wish! If faced with the choice, you would all take the soup!" Rolling her eyes, she flounced off.

"Huh?" asked Sam, befuddled. He did not get the allusion.

"C'mon, Sam, don't you know the one about the girl who is given as a birthday gift to Miltie in Miami?"

"No, I don't think so."

"Well, she rings Miltie's doorbell, and when he opens the door she takes a provocative pose and announces, '*Super sex*!'

"Miltie looks at her for a minute, and he replies, 'I think I'll take the soup.'"

The guys all snickered and looked at Sam expectantly. He squinted his eyes in thought and then shook his head. "I *still* don't get it."

"Sam, Sam, the old guy thinks she is offering *s-o-u-p or sex*—now do you get it?"

"Oh, yeah, yeah, I get it," said Sam, slapping Sy on the back.

"Uh-oh," muttered Sy to Max, "this guy has mud for brains. No way Mitzi will stick with him for much longer. She is one smart cookie, and I can't believe she's that desperate."

"Good news for me," growled Max. "I have been paying a lot of attention to Gladys who won't give me the time of day, but maybe I would have a chance with Mitzi—whaddya think?"

Sy watched Max adjust his wig as he leered at the girls' table, and he shook his head in wonder at Max's lack of self-consciousness.

Max had been a respected, successful lawyer in his day, and he was still well read and up to speed on many subjects. But these days he acted the fool whenever the girls were around.

How lucky for me, he thought, *to have Dottie by my side. She keeps me grounded, she really listens to me, and at the same time she gets me to do all these things I have never done before. She makes me feel vital and confident.* He smiled to himself ironically. *Even without the super sex.*

He mused about his friends and wondered if they were all caricatures of silly old men. Well, they were a decent bunch to joke and play cards with, but he could take just so much of them. He looked at his watch and realized he had to grab Dottie, as they were scheduled to go on the house tour that raised money for Good Samaritan Hospital ("Good Sam" to those who visited as often as they did).

"Dot," he called as he went to gather her up from the girls' table. "We don't want to be late." Their philanthropy was generous but practical. To be named "patrons" of the house tour, he had donated $5,000, enabling them to cut the long lines of common donors, have their names prominently printed in the program, and of course ensure that Good Sam would have private rooms for them when the time came.

"If I didn't think it would tire me out, I would've gone on that tour," said Flossy. "I adore looking at how other people decorate their homes and how they live. Norman and I always used to go, and I always brought home good ideas."

"You know that house from last month's *Architectural Digest*—the one Judith Thurman wrote about? I would give my eye teeth to see that one," said Faith.

"Do you mean the one that looked like an Aman hotel in Southeast Asia, with all the incredible statuary?" asked Mitzi. "I stayed at Amandari in Bali with my second husband—I think it was him, anyway. It was extremely sensuous," she recalled, getting dreamily lost in her memory.

"Yes, that's the one, and I agree with Faith," asserted Flossy. "It was truly an extraordinary spread. I rarely read the articles in detail, but as the house was in Palm Beach, I did."

"I always read them," declared Betty. "But then again, I'm a fast reader, so I can read everything."

"Oh, for God's sake, Betty, we *know* you are great at everything. Except modesty."

"But did you read that Thurman called the owners 'a low-key couple'? How can you be low-key with statues that are as tall as a house and a house that is twenty-eight thousand square feet?" inquired Babs, who, as always, remembered the numbers.

"Well, they do have grandchildren."

"Oh, for God's sake, do you know how big twenty-eight thousand square feet is?" asked Babs impatiently.

"Yes, we can count too, Babs," replied Flossy. "It is bigger than all seven of our apartments put together, but it doesn't mean I am not interested in *seeing* it. I don't want to *live* in it. Well, maybe for just a little while I would."

"Oh, Floss," said Babs, "what has happened to your socialist leanings? Aren't you the one who always tells us ad infinitum about your wonderful father who cast the only vote in town for Norman Thomas until Roosevelt espoused all his ideas?"

They all laughed, including Flossy, thinking back at how times had changed.

"Well, it's a new day. I remember when our business was small, and Mel and I could not even afford a vacation," reminisced Betty.

"*Our* business? You mean your husband and his brother's business, don't you?" Faith asked pointedly.

"Well, of course, literally it was the men's, but I always thought of myself as being a part of it. Didn't you, Floss? Really, didn't you, Babs?"

"Well, of course we did, because we didn't have any careers of our own. Our job was to be there for them when they came home, to share their troubles, to help them strategize and figure out how to grow the business...so we did feel as if we were part of it. Could they have done it without us? Probably yes. But I must say that Harold thought I was faster with the numbers than anyone. He thought that's why I always beat him at gin! Just think, if I were a young woman today, I could've been a partner at Deloitte & Touche," answered Babs.

I agree with you, Babs and Betty," said Flossy. "I hated housework, I was terrible at doing crafty things with my kids, and so what did I do? Certainly not, not, not cooking."

"Flossy, the take-out queen!" they all chorused.

Flossy acknowledged the toast, but went on in a more pensive vein. "Building the business was much more interesting than my daily life. I felt so useful when Norman and I struggled over a difficult problem he was having at work. I'm sure I helped him discern the forest from the trees—you know, take a longer view. As he was more inductive, and I am more deductive, I believe I complemented his thinking. In hindsight, it was immensely satisfying to see Norman succeed. As for me, I'm not sure I would have wanted to face those challenges every morning, day in and day out, like he did. But a part of me did long for something important, for something I could dig my teeth into, you know, to get my brain stimulated. I wonder what I could have been?"

"Inductive, reductive, deductive...you are being so philosophical, Flossy."

"Faith, you were the only one of us who actually had a job—well, sort of a part-time job, working in your husband's office. Did you mind being the receptionist to the great doctor?" asked Betty. "Or did you feel useful?"

"I'm not sure anymore," answered Faith. "When he was starting out, he could hardly afford an office, much less a receptionist. I was glad to be there for him. I would have done anything for him. And I practically *did* anything for him, all his life, but he was the one who got all the adoration—and frankly, he deserved it—but I was a wee, wee bit jealous, I think."

"Just a wee, wee bit?" repeated Betty sardonically. "I don't know which is worse, a husband who was a saint or one who was an oaf like mine."

The girls were used to Betty maligning her poor, sweet, departed husband, and they did not disagree with her, but as was her wont, her resentment came out in maligning someone else as well—this time Faith's husband, of all people.

They went on to wonder what they might have been had they not been housewives, and like their daughters, they had to manage careers and husbands and children.

Too late to change…and would they have wanted it?

"Okay," queried Mitzi, "if you were young now, what would you want to be? Let's go around the table. You first, Faith."

"I have no regrets, really. I have loved my life."

"C'mon, Faith, not one tiny regret?"

"Well, maybe, but I don't mourn over it. However, I will admit, walking with my daughter in Harvard Yard, I could see myself there as a young woman. But here is what I mean about no regrets. When the Depression hit, my father could only afford four years of college for my sister and me. He told my sister she had had her two, and now it was my turn. 'No, Papa,' I said, 'let Anne finish, and at least one of us will have a college degree.' Well, he listened to me, and it turned out for the best. I married, and after a few years I didn't *have* to work. My sister didn't marry and needed to work all her life, and in fact went on to get a graduate degree. She would not have been able to do that if she had given up her place to me."

"Gee, Faith, that was so unselfish of you," exclaimed Betty. And in a rare moment of public self-reflection, she admitted, "I don't think I would have done it, I really don't."

"Oh, it was not so self-sacrificing at the time. I was having a gay old time as a single girl in New York, but in hindsight, maybe, just maybe, I could've gotten to Harvard before parents' weekend."

"Hey, what happened to my game?" cried Mitzi. "Enough introspection."

"Okay, I'll be Golda Meir," announced Flossy. "If I get to choose, I might as well aim high. I wouldn't mind being one of the greatest figures of our century, and I would still get to meet you all when you came to Israel!"

They laughed and moved on to the next.

"Okay, since we are aiming high," announced Babs, "I'll go from partner at Deloitte to secretary of the Treasury!"

"Hooray for Babs," they cheered.

"Me, I'll be Nancy Pelosi," said Mitzi. "Not only does she get to be the boss of all those men in the House, but her husband buys Armani suits for her!"

Dottie's chair was empty, but they chose for her president of the Rockefeller Foundation, as she loved to give money away. She could never convince them to give to every one of her charities, so as head of Rockefeller, she could stop asking them and be very, very important.

Faith chose, as they suspected she would, "I'd like to be a doctor and take care of all you old bats."

Betty, no surprise, chose "CEO of Goldman Sachs!" and rubbed her hands together counting all her money.

And Gladys, lost in thought, was last. "I think I would just like to be beautiful," she said very quietly.

"Why do you always denigrate yourself, Gladys?" asked Mitzi. "You are a fine-looking woman. I mean, who of us is Sophia Loren?"

"Right!" added Flossy adamantly. "In fact, I saw Sophia Loren being interviewed once on the *Today Show* or one of those talk shows, long ago. I used to quote her all the time to Norman when I felt underappreciated. She, of all people, said, 'You can never tell a woman too often how beautiful she is!' Even she needed the reassurance."

"I *guess* that makes me feel better," replied Gladys hesitantly. "It's just that old feelings are hard to overcome. My husband always made it clear I was *not* Sophia Loren—hardly. The best he ever said was that I was…comfy in bed. Don't snicker. That was his idea of a compliment. I'd get all done up to go to a party, and for all the attention he paid, I could have been wearing a housecoat. You know, stuff like that. It was not that he was nasty or anything, more like he was oblivious or something. So I guess living all those years with him, I gave up trying.

"His not paying attention to how I *looked* made a big difference in those days before women's lib. I thought I was smart and competent—you all know I am—but I lost a lot of confidence in those days, thinking no man would really care for me."

The girls were rarely so revealing about the dark moments of their marriages or their feelings of insecurity. As Gladys looked around at her friends' widened eyes, she began to backpedal. "Don't get me wrong. It's not that we had a *bad* marriage, it was just a missing piece, that's all, I guess."

Frances, who had come to pick up Flossy, was listening to the conversation. She put her arms around Gladys and whispered how beautiful she was, and then she proclaimed to the girls, "My turn! I choose to be one of you!"

They all laughed and broke up for the day. Only one of them was really changing her life.

CHAPTER SIXTEEN

"My candle burns at both ends,
It will not last the night,
But ah, my foes, and oh, my friends,
It gives a lovely light."
— Edna St. Vincent Millay

Flossy recited her favorite poem as she reflected on yesterday's conversations with the girls. She had worked hard all her life to wring every ounce of joy out of every day. She knew everyone liked being with her because of her positive attitude, but what if she had used that energy for a more important goal? Well, she was not vain enough to think she could have been Golda Meir, but maybe she could have worked for the equitable society her father had espoused, maybe she could have excelled at something other than bridge, maybe...

Oh well, her candle was burning low, and...

At that moment, Flossy was jolted out of her reverie by the sound of sirens. She jumped up and ran out to her terrace to watch the ambulance speeding down the street. "Oh dear!" she exclaimed to Frances. "I always worry that they're coming for someone I know. It's turning into the building next door. I know so many people who live there."

"Flossy! Mrs. *Kane*!" yelled Frances as she grabbed hold of her and pulled her back to the breakfast table. "Stop being such a worrywart, and if you run outside like that again you're going to give me a heart attack! And then *you* will have to call an ambulance for *me*!"

They both laughed at the idea and together enjoyed the warm sunshine streaming through the picture windows while they dabbled at their breakfasts and perused the *Palm Beach Post* and the *New York Times.* The morning hours moved lazily by.

This time the doorbell interrupted their relaxation. When Frances opened the door to find Roberto standing there, his shoulders slumped, his hair unkempt, and his face drawn and haggard, she was so filled with compassion for him, she enveloped him in her arms and just held him.

"You've been working on that Wendy's case, haven't you, *mi amor*?"

"It makes my blood run cold," confessed Roberto. "I just can't get my mind around a man who walks into a restaurant in the middle of the day, nicely dressed in a coat and tie, and then pulls out a gun and tries to kill as many people as he can, and then he kills himself. I don't even get to put him away…maybe it's better. It would've been hard for me to be objective.

"I just can't help thinking of the poor guy he shot dead, a man who just walked back into the place because he forgot to pick up Wendy's free toy for his daughter when they left. What if he had *not* forgotten, what if he decided she didn't need another toy? What if…what if?"

As he buried himself in Frances's arms once more, Flossy walked in, and they pulled apart, Roberto embarrassed by his vulnerability and Frances by her lack of professionalism.

"Oh, *pardon* me." Flossy smiled as she turned away. "Go right back to what you were doing. Don't mind me!"

"We don't mind you, Flossy. I'm going to make Roberto a cup of coffee. Come join us on the terrace."

Frances brought out coffee and rolls, and ham and cheese and tomatoes and avocado, noting, "It is not only Jewish mothers who think eating will make you feel better. I just wish I had some chicken soup to feed you, *mi amigo*. Or *arroz con pollo*!"

Flossy told Roberto, "I would take Frances's *arroz con pollo* any day over the proverbial chicken soup. I am inviting you to dinner here with both of us…but I go to sleep very, very early," she said slyly.

Roberto and Frances, embarrassed by Flossy's implication, turned back to the subject of crime. "So, have you found out anything about this murdering nut case?" asked Frances.

"We know who he was and where he lived. We're going through his apartment now and examining everything on his computer, trying to find out if it was planned or if he just snapped."

"But what good does that do you now?" inquired Flossy. "The deed has been done."

"Actually, the more we can learn about crazy people like him, the more likely we are to prevent horrific crimes like this one. We look for patterns of behavior. For instance, what if we find he had been arrested six times in the past for minor infractions, but they were against property, and they were all restaurants? Or what if they were crimes against society, like defacing public buildings or breaking up peaceful gatherings? What if his apartment is filled with books about rage? He frequents websites that rail against our country? The medical examiner will even analyze his brain to see if he can find any anomalies. If we see any kind of pattern, we can begin to profile, and we just might take a more careful look at the next guy who gets arrested for breaking the windows of the firehouse or whatever."

Roberto slumped in his chair, knowing his quest would probably be useless. But knowing he had to continue, he started to get up.

"How about some dessert?" tempted Frances. "We have some delicious carrot cake!"

"Carrot cake—oh *Dios mio.* Being in the company of you lovely ladies, I almost forgot why I came here." Noting Frances's furrowed brow and down-turned mouth, he continued, "Of course I came for comfort to the person I care about most, but I also came to bring you some sad news. Your friend Paula who lives down the street was found dead this morning by her visiting nurse. I am so sorry."

"I knew those sirens signaled something ominous," Flossy cried out. But in a more sober voice, she said softly, "I'm not surprised. She should not have been living alone. What did she do, take too many pills?"

"Exactly! At least, that's what we think for now. We have to wait for the autopsy to be sure. But how did you know?"

"Paula was always mixing up her pills. She resisted having someone help her out, except for the visiting nurse who came once a week to fill up her little pill containers. There was a period of time when she was sleeping all day and staying up all night because she reversed her pills. Then, when was it—a few weeks ago, Frances? She almost killed us driving through a red light on Worth Avenue. Poor, poor Paula, she was so stubborn."

Frances stared down at the table. Squeezing her eyes shut, she massaged her temples. "When did she die?" she asked.

"We think she died Saturday night, but as no one visited her yesterday, I won't be sure until I hear from the medical examiner's office. Why do you ask like that?"

"Because I was there Friday afternoon, and I was *arranging her pills for her.*"

"Tell me, Frances, love, what happened?"

Frances looked up at Roberto and related the story of her summoning and how the pills had been knocked from their containers all over the floor. "They asked if I would come over to help them put the pills back in the right order. Of course I agreed, but

I didn't think I was really needed. After all, the directions on the bottles are all very clear. Anyway, I popped over, helped them pick up the pills, found the bottles where Paula told us they were, in a cabinet above the refrigerator, followed the directions, and laid them all out. Then I left, but I did not leave her alone. Our friend was still there with her."

"Did you say Paula knew where the pill bottles were?"

"Yes, she did. She kept saying, 'They think they are hiding them from me, but I am more observant than they think.' Do you think I'm going to get in trouble for this? Really, I was just being nice."

"Absolutely not, my pigeon. But tell me, what sleeping pills did you give her?"

"I did not *give* her any sleeping pills! I do not like the way you are saying that. I put the Ambien that was all over the floor in the containers for Friday, Saturday, and Sunday in the space for ten p.m.!" Frances folded her arms adamantly under her breasts and stamped her feet.

Roberto was amused and beguiled. "No, no, no—I'm sorry I said that badly. As a policeman, I should be more careful of my words, but it seems there was an almost empty bottle of Restoril, which is so much stronger than Ambien, in that cabinet as well, and I just wondered if you gave her that, or..."

"*I did not!* I gave her the pills that were on the floor. I brushed them off and put them back where they belonged, as I have now told you *three* times."

"I know, I know, but I just had to ask. We are surmising at this point that, as you just said, Paula knew where her meds were kept and got them down for herself. We also found an empty bottle of oxycodone in the wastepaper basket. Furthermore, maybe, Flossy, she was not so confused as you think."

Roberto pulled out his notebook, and read, "'Sweetheart, I am having a huge piece of the most delicious carrot cake for dinner, looking out over the ocean, and I am as happy as I can ever be.

I would not mind if I died tonight. I love you.'" Roberto sighed. "This is the message she left on her daughter's voice mail."

Flossy, who had been pacing, sat down. "Oh, Frances, Roberto, this is so sad. I don't think Paula would have snuffed out her own candle, but if she did, at least she was not in pain or misery."

"'Snuffed her own candle,' that's so poetic, Flossy," said Frances admiringly.

"It is an interpretation of a poem," said Flossy, lost in thought.

Frances and Roberto tiptoed to the door and made up before he left.

CHAPTER SEVENTEEN

"Some cause happiness wherever they go;
others whenever they go."
— Oscar Wilde

The girls were lunching as usual before the Thursday bridge game. Having lost three friends in as many weeks, they started out somber but soon began to giggle and chatter at one another as they talked about their frailties, their clothes, their fears, their children, and their memories, in no special order. It was, as always, a group stream of consciousness.

Marty, the real estate mogul, approached the table. "Good afternoon, girls," he said, greeting each of them and squeezing their shoulders. This was his idea of endearing himself, although most of them knew he was picturing their apartments while making small talk. "Does anyone, by any chance, have the phone number of either of Paula's daughters? I would love to call and offer my condolences. She was such a sweet soul." The treacle was oozing, and they all knew he wanted to get his hands on her apartment to sell.

"Offer your services is more like it." Betty smiled brightly back at him.

"Well, of course, of course, that too, but..."

"Sorry, Marty, we don't have any idea. Why don't you camp out in front of 2500 South Ocean Boulevard and flag them down when they come to close the apartment next week," said Betty, cutting him off. She got a jab in the kidney from Faith.

"Don't mind Betty, Marty," said Faith. "She's just upset, as all of us are, about Paula's death. It's just a bit unseemly to be thinking of selling her apartment this minute, don't you think? A word of advice: be a little discreet, okay?"

He bobbed his head in mute agreement and scurried away with as much dignity as he could muster. The girls all laughed and breathed a sigh of relief to be rid of him.

"Here we are in the twenty-first century, and we have our own little Dickens scenario. It's almost as if he is rubbing his palms together, gleefully thinking of the money he'll make as we all die. God, he is so unctuous," declared Babs.

"I'm not sure I know what that means," said Gladys, "but it sure sounds like his margarine personality."

"You have got it exactly right, Gladys, dear. Uriah Heep was Dickens's most famous unctuous character. You can look him up on Google," encouraged Flossy.

"You mean on the computer?" asked Gladys. "You have to be kidding. My kids bought me an Apple, I think it's called, and I don't have the faintest idea what to do with it. *They* use it when they come down. I honestly think they bought it for themselves."

Babs chastised, "Gladys, I don't believe you. I know you know how to *shop* online; you've told me you watch for the sales."

"I know how to do *that*," dithered Gladys. "But I don't do that interactive stuff. I mean I can go to the website and see if there is a sale, but then I go to the store, you know?"

Babs looked skeptical, but let the weak explanation pass. "Well, as for me, every day we don't play bridge together, I do play Sudoku online. It keeps me sharp, and it keeps me company, if you know what I mean."

"I do know what you mean," added Mitzi. "Have you ever gone online to J-Date? I have met several very nice men there, nicer and smarter than that goof who Sy brought here from Boca."

"Wait, wait! There are two interesting things you just said," jumped in Flossy. "You are meeting *men* online? *And* you are no longer dating Sy's friend Sam?"

"He is not *really* Sy's friend," interrupted Dottie. "Sy has told me that he hardly knew him—he was a friend of his cousin's, and I'm glad you said that, Mitzi, dear, because Sy thinks he is an idiot!"

"Well, he is good-intentioned, but he is just so dumb, and he has no sense of humor. I need a man who is at least smart enough to get jokes. I don't care about his looks too much—at our age that would be asking for too much—and he doesn't need to drive, because I do. I don't mind if they are rich, though."

"We know y'all don't *mind* if they're rich," interjected Betty in her best imitation of Mitzi's southern drawl. It was a funny caricature, but predictably, it had a mean undertone.

"But tell us more about your J-Dates," begged Gladys, suddenly getting more interested in using her computer for something other than shopping.

"Well, I haven't actually gone *out* with one yet," said Mitzi, "but I have been carrying on some very interesting conversations. One guy who is from Atlanta is coming here for a few weeks at the Breakers next month. I am very excited to meet him. He sounds so kind and funny, so sophisticated, but sweet. His picture is probably twenty years old, but as I said before, I don't really care about looks anymore. But he is rich," she said with a smile. "I googled him."

"You want to hear arrogance, let me tell you who I met when I went on the J-Date website," said Babs.

"*You*?" interrupted Faith. "I thought you just use the computer for playing Sudoku. You seem so reserved, Babs, how come you did it?"

"First, let me tell you I did it only once. I just wanted to see the site between games," she admitted. "And I meet this guy who is a big bridge player and golfer, so he *says*. And then he writes to me: 'If you want to learn more about me, just google me, I come up *first* under Wolfenstein.' Such ego. I never googled him, and I never went back. I can fend just fine on my own."

"Well, actually, if you google my elder son," bragged Betty, "he comes up first under Kantrowitz."

"*Aaggh*, Betty," snorted Babs, "I just said how arrogant that is, and there you go..."

"I can't help it if it's true."

Faith and Flossy broke the thread before it got pulled too tight and started talking about their e-mailing daughters—how busy they were that they could not talk on the phone but stayed in touch with them online. "I actually like to hear my daughter's voice," said Flossy, "so *I* call *her*, but with my grandchildren it's the best way to keep in touch, especially the ones who live overseas. Even my great-granddaughters in Boston are sending me e-mails now—with pictures of themselves and their projects. I feel as if I am still a part of their lives."

"And do you know, I'm playing Scrabble on Facebook with my granddaughter," said Faith, proudly announcing that she was probably the oldest person on Facebook.

"Faith, you are always so *au courant*. How do you do that?" asked Flossy. "I would love to try it."

"Wait till your kids come down, and they will set you up. Or if my kids come first, they'll come over and do it for you, and you can surprise yours."

"Oh, I love that idea," said Flossy, bouncing in anticipation. "Do you twitter too?"

"The verb is 'tweet,' Floss, but no, I don't have a group I really want to be a part of...except you all of course. But I do text with my girls."

"Wow, Faithie! Who would have thunk it...our own octogenarian geek!"

But suddenly changing moods, Flossy asked the group, "Speaking of daughters, did you all hear about Paula's last message to her daughter on the phone?"

"We did," they all exclaimed at once. They rehashed Paula's last known moments...spilling her pills, Frances's help in putting them all back in the containers, the passion for pecan pie and carrot cake. They were all nattering at each other, wondering if Paula really was *compos mentis* enough to commit suicide, or if her message was just coincidental to her overdosing. They would never know. In their effort to try and understand, to avoid acknowledging that it could one day be one of them, Frances's name came up over and over again. Did she really know what she was doing? After all, Frances was not a trained RN, just a Puerto Rican home-care aide, with no real degree. Could it have been Frances's mistake?

Flossy was stupefied by their desire to point the blame at someone else, someone who was not one of them.

Flossy fumed, but before she could jump into the conversation, one of the other girls did, praising Frances with faint condemnation. "Frances was a godsend. Paula was so upset and anxious when I accidentally spilled her pills, I knew she wouldn't be content to let me put them back. Frances was so calming and in control—she does not have to be a *trained* nurse to have that effect. Paula, and I, we were grateful to have someone who really knew what she was doing take charge. I *thought* Frances handled the situation very well. She breezed in, scooped the pills back into their correct spots, hugged and consoled Paula, and she scooted out. It was all done in *ten* minutes. I never could have calmed Paula *and* figured it out so quickly. Who of us could?"

She could not believe her luck. With all her brilliant planning, she could never have imagined this scenario. Paula, dear Paula, virtually leaving a suicide note. And just on the outside chance that the suicide motive didn't fly in the long run, she had laid the groundwork to set up Frances. She was surely home free.

The girls all clucked in assent, but a few raised their eyebrows, not completely convinced that Frances was not culpable. Flossy saw no point in making it more of an issue. Not now, anyway.

CHAPTER EIGHTEEN

"There is really no evidence 'that people in this country or in yours are any sleepier than their parents.' We just talk about it more."

— Jim Horne, director of the Sleep Research Center at Loughborough University, England

Flossy has been uncharacteristically quiet all through the game, although she was, characteristically, winning.

Babs could not understand how Flossy, who now played far less than she did, could still be the big money winner. Babs won consistently too, but she had to admit that Flossy rarely made a mistake. What an ideal partner Flossy was; they always won when they played together in the club tournaments, even though they were getting to be the *senior* senior citizens. Lately some of the young locals had been cleaning up at the duplicate games in town. What had Sy said at last week's competition? "Those kids are only in their twenties—for God's sake, I have ties that old."

Meanwhile, as if the girls had been reading Babs's thoughts, they began discussing the latest issue of *Bridge Week*. They all subscribed and all practiced the new conventions at their weekly bridge lesson. But each year it got harder and harder to stay up to date.

Remembering the cards played in each hand had always come naturally to each of them. Betty recalled trying to help her son when he first started. "'Mom,' he said to me, 'how can you possibly remember every card in every trick?'

"'How can you *not*?' I answered him. He took umbrage, and I don't think he ever played again. I can't think why. I was just telling him the truth."

"Oh, for God's sake, Betty, not *everyone* has the same powers of concentration that we do, but they can still enjoy the game," reproved Mitzi. "I remember my last husband played with a group of men in our cabana every Sunday afternoon. They were not of our caliber, but they laughed and had fun."

"Sy adored that group," added Dottie. "He sorely misses them. Not that he does not enjoy being with me and going out into society more, but there was a certain special moment in time he shared with those guys, and it is a poignant loss for him."

"My husband was in that group. As I recall, they dubbed themselves, ironically and correctly, the 'Dummy Club,'" scoffed Betty. "Why is it that they could remember every dirty joke they ever heard and every football score and batting average, but not when to bid two spades?"

"Oh, Betty, you act so superior, but it is all a matter of interest. They played for fun and relaxation; we play seriously. I would say we are semiprofessional," said Gladys.

"Hardly semiprofessional." Faith laughed at the elevation of their skills. "But I agree, we do take it seriously, because if you play as often as we do, for as many years as we have, it sure would be boring not to advance or change the way we play. And in all candor, I still think it is a bit boring, and I bet you all do too. What do you think of the idea of taking up a new pastime?"

"Oh sure," suggested Betty sarcastically, "let's study physics."

"*Oy*," said Gladys, fluttering her eyelashes, "I'd rather learn how to J-Date."

"I think we should have an investment club," proposed Babs.

"With whose money?" asked Mitzi. "Ours? You don't know what we can afford."

"Puh-leez, Mitzi, I know you can afford to live down here and buy more clothes than anyone I know, and…"

"And I suggest we get back to bridge," said Flossy, counting her money.

They all watched her and wondered how she did it. She was half deaf, often missed a bid if they didn't speak up, but she always won. "We know you want to get back into the game so you can win some more," teased Faith. "How do you do it so consistently?"

All ears were waiting, especially Babs's, who admired Flossy's skill but still chafed at her winnings.

"Okay, it's time, I guess, to share my secret, because I love you all. It's—ESP! I can read the cards when they are upside down!"

"*Really*?" blurted out Gladys, wide-eyed. Some thought her naïveté was often put on. But not this time. She went on, "I heard that this is possible, that they did these experiments at Duke, and then I read about others in that book, *Blink*—but you are joking, right, Floss?"

"We all have heard about people 'reading' cards, Gladys, but yes, as you well know, I am joking. My secret has always been this. I read *Bridge Week* in bed just before I am ready to go to sleep, and I truly believe that sleeping on the information embeds it in my memory. I have done this instinctively forever, since high school at least. And recently I saw on *60 Minutes* that it has been scientifically proven to be true! These kids who do all-nighters to study for exams do a lot less well than those who study right before bed and get a good night's sleep. Our sons and daughters who are working for law firms and investment banks and doing deals until all hours of the morning would be sharper if they went home and went to sleep."

"But they can't, Flossy. You know that. With communications what they are today, these deal negotiations go almost twenty-four hours a day. My grandson who works at a big New York law firm once worked forty-five days straight without a break, almost eighteen hours a day. But the opposing firm was doing the same thing. Neither one would back down and say, 'Let's take the weekend off.' Rather than the most intelligent thing to do, it would be taken as a sign of weakness, according to my grandson. When I asked him what would happen if he went home one night and spent it with his new and lonely wife, he told me that if he did, there would be six associates right behind him hungrier and willing to work twice as hard as he was. It's a real dilemma," interjected Dottie.

"And I bet he makes a fortune, and he doesn't even have time to spend it!"

"Exactly!"

"Poor kids…what a life they have these days."

"And bringing the conversation full circle, they all hire 'sleep consultants' for their children."

"Huh?"

"Really, I read this in the *New York Times*," claimed Faith. "It seems these kids work so hard that they get home at night and are too tired and feel too guilty to discipline their children—especially the mothers, whose job it was for generations. So what happens is they let their toddlers call the shots and stay up late and do what they want, including *sleeping with their parents—ALL NIGHT*. The phenomenon actually has a name: 'co-sleeping.' Could you die? The fathers drag themselves out of the master bedroom and wind up going to sleep in the children's princess and airplane beds…you know what I mean, and the children stay in the king-size beds with the moms. When the situation becomes untenable they hire a specialist, of course. The specialists have to *teach* the parents how to put their kids to bed. Did you ever?"

Half of the girls were agog at this report and found it unbelievable.

But Flossy and Mitzi concurred. They had read the same article. "In fact," said Flossy, "my daughter Zoë knows one of the couples profiled in the article. Zoë is a good friend of their mother, who has been so proud, and rightfully so, of her kids' accomplishments. Her kids never *needed* to work and could have lounged around all day doing nothing but playing cards, like us. But instead this young woman became a very successful entrepreneur, and in the article she said something like, 'I had a lot of serious boundaries when I was growing up. Now I think there's a backlash.' Can you imagine how her mother feels now, getting blamed because her daughter can't put her kids to bed?"

"Her mother must be thinking, my daughter is ambitious and smart, and she gets in the *New York Times* not for her accomplishments, but because she can't get her children to go to bed. And this is because I set serious boundaries? What is this world coming to?" asked Gladys, stating the obvious to them all.

"And if you read farther into the article—it was almost *two* full pages—it talks about the techniques the consultants advise for getting the kids to stay in their rooms. One of the best was to give their favorite stuffed animal a piece of the mother's clothing. Don't laugh now, it gets funnier. One little girl chose her mother's *bra*, and carried around her teddy bear wearing her mother's sexy number from Victoria's Secret or somewhere," added Faith.

"What do you know from Victoria's Secret, Faithie?" asked Dottie.

"More than you, Dottie. I can't afford La Perla!"

"And who can guess the end result?" asked Mitzi. "Putting aside that these little kids are going to be really screwed up, the parents never get to sleep together. The weaning from their bed is too exhausting for them, so they only try it once or twice a week. You can imagine how well that works. So even after being counseled how important it is to be firm and to give kids parameters, they give in and go to bed in separate rooms so they can get some sleep. They say—get this—that sleep is the new sex!"

"Well, it is for us, anyway," wisecracked Betty.

"At least we can use it to remember our bridge conventions… maybe even to remember what we did last week."

But someone remembered very well what she did last week.

CHAPTER NINETEEN

"Great minds think alike."
— Unattributed

Flossy had been distracted from her feelings of anxiety by the bridge game and amusing conversations, but now that she was back at home with Frances, she became quiet once more.

"What's up, honeybunch?" asked Frances.

"Oh, nothing, Frances, it's just that I'm tired. I had a long day."

"Yes, but I know you. What happened at the game today that's bothering you?" As Frances prodded Flossy's psyche, she also took her blood pressure and tested her oxygenation, which were both perfectly normal. "You don't need any oxygen, you are as normal as I am, ha ha, so that's not it. Tell me, what did you talk about?"

They sat on the terrace together, watching the pelicans swoop over the palm trees as the setting sun reflected in the gentle waves of the low tide. Frances was so considerate and attentive that Flossy's heart was filled with love for this competent woman who had come into her life. Flossy had dreaded the thought of giving up her independence, and she still hated the concept, but the reality was very clear to her. She needed Frances, and she was so very, very fortunate to have her. How could her friends even *consider* that Frances had anything to do with Paula's death, how did they *dare*? She would die; she would *want* to die if she did not have Frances. She shook herself out of her maudlin thoughts and chose instead to amuse Frances by relating the conversations at the bridge game.

"So I won as usual—twenty dollars. Everyone wanted to know how I consistently win when I don't play as often as I used to, and I can't even hear the bids. I told them I have ESP; I use my extrasensory perception to *read* the cards!"

"Oh, Flossy, how funny of you. But you know, I think there is some truth in ESP. I think I have it sometimes. It's like I know when a patient is not doing well in the night, even though they haven't called out to me—like Miss Clavell in *Madeleine.*"

"Frances, did you have *Madeleine* growing up in Puerto Rico?"

"I did—in Spanish! It was my favorite book when I was a child, and I read it to my girls, and now they read it to their children. I don't know what it is about that book, whether it's the rhythm of the words or the bright colors or the cuteness of the story, but despite Madeleine going to the *hospital*, kids do not feel scared. As a girl, I used to drown in the illustrations. Someday, Madame La Kane, we have to go to Paris together!"

"That's a deal, Frances. It is so interesting that you loved that book so much. Zoë did too. In fact, when she had to do a French project she wrote and illustrated a new Madeleine story that she made up...she was only in junior high school...and since then she has always been entranced by Paris. And now with my grandson and his family living there..."

"Flossy, the stars are clearly aligned for us to travel to Paris!"

"Well, we shall see, *Francoise.* Maybe if I could get off oxygen every night..."

"What, you don't think they breathe oxygen in Paris, my love?"

"Of course, of course, I just want to feel a little more confident in my health. Maybe next summer."

"Well, not if you are going to get rid of *me*, Flossy, my love. I won't allow it," threatened Frances, shaking her finger in mock discipline.

Flossy swore she would never go without Frances, and the discipline reminded her of the co-sleeping discussion. She recounted the article to Frances, and they didn't know whether to laugh or cry.

"But you know," added Frances, "it is not just working mothers. Even stay-at-home moms today are afraid to discipline their children. I don't get it, either. How could they not know that a child who has boundaries is more fun to be with? You know, the best-behaved child in my family up until two years ago was my son's dog."

Flossy started to laugh, but Frances wasn't kidding. "My son got a dog during his last year of law school, and not to be trite, but this animal became his best friend. This is my reading child, and he read up on how to raise a dog, and he practiced all the behavioral techniques on Sophilita from when she was a puppy. They had a great time together, and she was never a pain, because she listened. So last year, when he and his wife had their first baby, I had a feeling they would treat the baby the same, and guess what—I was right. Their little girl gets *one* story read to her and goes to bed—lights out, door closed, no crying. She is my angel. The others? *Dios mio*, they run around like mongrels until they drop, and then they get carried to bed. My solution is that all prospective parents should get a dog the year before they get pregnant, practice on the dog, see that the dog will love you even when you say *no*, and then have a baby!"

"Dr. Spock, I love the idea. We should write to the *New York Times*!"

"Well, that can be our project for tomorrow, but you are avoiding telling me what is on your mind," Frances prompted.

"Okay, okay, Frances, you are right. I just can't stand people sometimes..."

"Uh-oh. It's about me, isn't it?"

"You are so canny, Frances. I think you *do* have ESP. When our friend who called you over to Paula's related what happened there, she praised you, but left just a tiny opening, a tiny wedge of possibility that you could be suspected of...of mixing up the pills. She didn't actually say it in any way. I'm not sure she even meant to do it, but the suggestion of carelessness kind of hung there in the air. Perhaps the girls just want to suspect that an immigrant, someone different from themselves, was responsible. No one actually came out and *said* anything, but I felt it. I felt it strongly, and I was so upset, I couldn't even talk. And that is *not* like me. Once we started playing bridge, I got caught up in the game as I always do, and I kind of forgot about it, but the feeling is back, and I shouldn't be sharing it with *you*, because I don't want you to hate my girlfriends, but now I've done it. And so while I'm sharing what I shouldn't, I also think there is something fishy—no pun intended—about Bunny's death and Paula's. The same person was the last one to see each of them alive. I can't believe I'm even articulating this thought. I must be reading too many mysteries... so ignore that, please." Flossy waved her hand back and forth in front of her face as if to banish the thought.

"For starters, *muchacha*, don't worry so much about me. This business has given me a thick skin, you better believe it. You think everyone treats me like you do? No, no, no, my Flossy. I have been treated like a doormat, like a slave, like a sex object...believe me, I have experienced it all. *Todos*! You worry because you *infer* that your friends suspect me of making a mistake. I have been in jobs where people talk about me when I am right in the room, when I have taken good care of their rotten old mother and cleaned up after her and then made dinner for the whole family, and then they sit at the table talking about what I have done wrong, as if I am not even there.

"I have been chased around the house by senile old men who want to get their last feel of a firm bootie, and I have been pawed

he would think of Roberto. *But, whoa, am I ever getting ahead of myself.* She pulled herself up short and stopped dreaming.

Common sense was her strong suit and she knew it. She knew when to cajole, when to be tough, when to back off with her patients. Flossy called it emotional intelligence. But with Roberto, it was hard to be so sensible. She feared she was falling in love. *What an old-fashioned idea*, she chided herself. But she wondered if he might be too, just a little.

This night she was working hard to help Roberto shed the horrors of the shooting at Wendy's, but she knew it was an uphill battle. So since his mind was on crime, she thought she just might be able to distract and amuse him by relating her conversation with Flossy.

Sipping her wine and munching on cheese and grapes, she told him of the suspicion that had been launched her way, and then casually put forth her theory. "I wonder if it isn't more suspicious that the *same* person was the last to be with, and *feed*, both Bunny and Paula." She succeeded in amusing, if not distracting him.

"*Oh, Ceesco*!" he laughed.

"*Yes, Pancho*," she giggled, loving their pet names from their favorite TV show as children, *The Cisco Kid*.

"You're reading too many mysteries," he echoed Flossy. "You're talking about a coincidence, not a *pattern*. And besides, what would be the motive?"

"You don't have a motive for the nut case at Wendy's." It slipped out before she could catch herself. "Oh my God, I am so sorry. I'm trying to distract you, and there I go being stupid."

"I forgive you, my pet. Sometimes the motive is so illogical, you get tragic events like Wendy's, but most often motive is the master key. You know the obvious ones—money, jealousy, power."

"I'll have to think about that."

Now Roberto tried to distract Frances in other ways, but she was still in pursuit of her idea. "You know, Flossy and I have seen her shopping a lot. Maybe she wanted their money."

"And just how would she have used their money?" asked Roberto, dismayed at her focus.

"We-e-e-ll, I know you are going to think this is really, really crazy, but right before Bunny died, we saw her shopping downtown and Flossy was *sure* she heard the salesgirl address *her* as Mrs. Boardman. She seemed to dash away when she saw us. I mean maybe this is hindsight, but maybe she was using Bunny's credit card."

"Now you are really being imaginative," murmured Roberto as he continued to distract her, this time quite successfully.

CHAPTER TWENTY-ONE

"Meesus Ka-eene, I am home!" No answer.

"Flossy, Flossy, where are you?" No answer.

Frances looked in the den. No one was there. She ran to the bedroom. No one was there. She peeked out onto the terrace. She looked in the bathrooms. She was not panicking, but she was feeling something like dread. The last thing she had heard as she walked out the door was Flossy on the phone, accepting a date, and saying something about her having a night off.

And then she noticed a light through the louvered door of Flossy's walk-in closet. She pulled at the door with unnecessary force and beheld a startled Flossy perusing her substantial collection of designer clothes.

"Flossy, you gave me a fright!"

"WHAT?"

"You gave me a scare!"

"WHAT are you SAYING?"

Frances realized that Flossy had taken out her hearing aids in preparation for bed and never even heard her come in. So she yelled that she was worried when she couldn't find Flossy and asked what she was doing in her closet at ten o'clock at night. "DO

YOU HAVE A LATE-NIGHT DATE?" she teased loudly as her heart rate returned to normal.

Flossy picked up her hearing aids from the night table and deftly inserted them in her ears so they could talk. "There, that's better. Now, why were you worried?"

"Nothing, nothing really," sighed Frances, giving Flossy a squeeze. "I think I am becoming paranoid. When I left I heard you on the phone accepting an invitation or something and saying I could use a night off, and I…I just was afraid that you-know-who had come over, and, and I had left you alone."

This time it was Flossy's turn to give Frances a reassuring hug. "Oh, Frances, my love, I do not want you to worry about me like that. We had a ridiculous conversation before you went out. I don't even want to think about it anymore."

"You are right," conceded Frances. "Roberto laughed at the idea. No more imaginative murder mystery plots! So who was on the phone, and what were you doing in the closet so late, if I may ask?"

"You may ask, and I will tell." Flossy grinned. "It was Gladys on the phone confirming the date of her birthday party next week at Canard D'Argent…la-di-dah!"

"And you were in the closet at ten o'clock deciding what to wear to the party!"

"Exactly. I had gotten all ready for bed, and I started to think about birthdays and parties and being old, and as I was getting maudlin, I decided to do something practical to divert myself. Then as I started to think it didn't matter what I wore, I am such an old bat, I remembered an old joke."

"So tell me the old joke."

"No, no, it's too silly." But Flossy had already started to laugh. "Okay, here goes—

"Lillian and Bernice, two widows, are talking. Lillian says, 'That nice Mr. Cohen just asked me out on a date. I know you went out with him last week. What was he like?'

"Bernice says, 'Well, let me tell you. He shows up at my apartment punctually at seven, dressed like such a *mensch*, in a fine suit, and he brings me such beautiful flowers! Then he takes me downstairs, and what's there but a luxury car, a limousine, no less, uniformed chauffeur and all. Then he takes me out for dinner, a marvelous dinner—lobster, champagne, the works. Then we go see a show. Let me tell you, Lillian, I enjoyed it so much I could have just died from pleasure! So then when we get back to my apartment he turns into an *animal*. Completely crazy, he tears off my expensive new dress and has his way with me two times!'

"Lillian says, '*Oy g'vald*...so I shouldn't go out with him?'

"Bernice says, 'No, no, no, dahlink, I'm just saying, don't wear a new dress!'"

Flossy had been acting out the story, and as she got to the punch line, she was laughing as much as Frances. Frances, who always loved a good Jewish joke, could not catch her breath. Flossy reached for her oxygen and pretended to administer it to Frances, and they both wound up hysterical all over again.

"So, my sweet, for Gladys's party, are you going to wear a new dress or a *schmatte*?" asked Frances.

"How do you know that word?" asked Flossy.

"Oh, Flossy, I have worked for enough Jewish families to know lots of Yiddish expressions."

"You know," reminisced Flossy. "There was a time I used to pretend not to understand any Yiddish at all. I was probably a bit embarrassed by my immigrant parents who, even after many years here, still had an 'haccent' and spoke in Yiddish when they didn't want us children to understand. Of course we always did understand. And once I became a teenager, I really tried to detach myself from their experience. Well, you know, Francie, I regret it now. I know so little of their lives before I was born. How I wish I had asked more about their lives in Russia, before they emigrated. I don't even know the names of the towns where they were born, not that they even exist anymore, I bet.

In any event, it is one of my regrets...and you know, Frances, I don't regret much. But remember when we saw that movie last year, *The Golden Door*, about the Italian immigrants? My parents could have been on that very same boat in those very same horrid conditions, and they never told us...never a word of complaint about any hardships they endured. And look at me, I whine at nothing!"

"Oh no, you do not. You are a tough and smart lady. You should only know from *vining*," Frances comforted in her very best Yiddish intonation.

Flossy laughed at Frances's Puerto Rican Yiddish cadence.

"Tell me more, Flossy. I love your stories."

"Well, my father did well. He had a dry goods store in Asbury Park, New Jersey, and..."

"You mean *the* Asbury Park, where Bruce Springsteen comes from?"

"I do. We lived in a tiny town just south of there called Bradley Beach. Each of my parents drove a big blue Packard. When my mother went to help my father in the store and left her car home, I would *steal* it and drive up and down the sandy streets. I was thirteen. There were hardly any other cars on the road, but can you imagine doing that now?

"My best friend and I would skip school all the time and go to the beach when the weather was warm—it was only two blocks away from my house—or shopping downtown in the winter. One day we were strolling around Steinbach's, the department store in Asbury Park, and who do we stroll right into? My mother! She was so mad she wouldn't even drive us home."

"That was your mother's idea of being mad?"

"Yes, she was such a gentle, loving person, that's about as angry as she ever got. But when my *father* got home, oh boy, did he holler. So I didn't do that again for...at least a month! I wasn't really frightened of my parents. They were so good to me, and I was a good daughter—willful, for sure, but good.

"Then I met Norman."

"Tell me, tell me," Frances pleaded while she helped Flossy into bed.

"I was sitting on the beach with a friend of mine, and I saw this *gorgeous* man walking out of the ocean. 'Who is *that*?' I asked my friend.

"'Oh, that's my cousin Norman. Do you want to meet him?'"

"'He's an *Adonis*,' I swooned. I was totally dazzled. I was only seventeen, and Norman was twenty-two, and after we were introduced, I was sure he would never call me, *but*...he called me that very night.

"The rest is history, a very, very long history," Flossy yawned.

"Tell me one more story," Frances begged.

"Well, now I'm thinking of us as young marrieds, and we belonged to a beach club called the East Side Casino." Flossy half closed her eyes as she pictured the scene. "It was quite glamorous, with cabanas and two pools and a beautiful beach. Sundays were long and lazy. We used to sit around my in-laws' cabana while the children all played around us. Then at four o'clock the music would start up. There was a small dance floor by the dining pavilion, and the children would beg us to dance. You would have loved it, Frances. It was a Latin combo with bongo drums and maracas and guitars. They played rumbas and tangos, and we swayed in our bathing suits, with the sun shining down on us, all sweaty and sexy, until the children would run between us, and I would dance with Michael, and Norman would dance with Zoë...and it was a sweet, sweet moment in time."

"Show me!" said Frances, grabbing Flossy. And they danced around the bedroom to an imaginary rumba, until Frances tucked Flossy in. She was already half asleep as Frances inserted the breathing tubes into her nose and turned on the oxygen machine that quietly accompanied her dreams. And Frances danced to her room, thinking of partnering with Roberto in a bathing suit on a tropical isle of her imagination.

CHAPTER TWENTY-TWO

"Bonsoir, Madame Kane!"

"Enchanté, Monsieur D'Argent."

Monsieur D'Argent greeted all the girls with great charm and élan, bending to kiss their hands and leading them, each as if she were his personal guest, to the table he had reserved for Gladys's birthday celebration. Always considerate of his guests, he had seated them as far away from the pianist as possible, while still not in Siberia. He knew the girls had trouble hearing in crowded rooms, but still they would want to enjoy the action. His restaurant was deservedly rated the best in Palm Beach. Some might say the food was a bit bland, as it catered to an elderly crowd, but it was the bland best nonetheless.

"How beautiful is this room! I just love the contrast of the raw brick walls with the extravagant flower arrangements and old-fashioned china and crystal. It is such a combination of chic and warmth," declared Gladys. "Every time I come here, I feel...well, I feel elegant."

"Is that from the room or from Monsieur D'Argent's attention?" snapped Betty, who noticed that everyone was getting the same attention she wished would be reserved for her.

"Betty, it's the combination of both," placated Faith. "Don't be irritable to Gladys on her birthday."

"Well, you're right, and this calls for another glass of champagne," allowed Betty. She had downed her first glass while the other girls had merely taken sips.

Eyebrows were raised all around as Dottie muttered, "At least she drove here herself. I wouldn't want any of us driving home with her."

Betty was, or acted, oblivious to her friends' consternation, and she toasted, "To the merry widows!"

"Who's so merry?"

"We are." Another toast.

"Well, kinda," added Mitzi. "I'd sure rather be a merry Wife of Windsor."

"Not me," answered Betty as she downed her champagne, "I'd rather be a merry mistress."

"Oooooh…whose?"

"There's the rub!"

"Enough with the Shakespeare, I'm starving, and if I don't eat soon, it will be a tragedy," said Flossy, egging them on.

"But, ah, perchance to dream…" quoted Betty as Monsieur D'Argent walked over to the table to personally take their orders.

As Gladys would be paying, they all ordered lavishly without regard to price, except Flossy, who chose two first courses. "Two first courses, Flossy, we thought you were starving!"

"Oh, Babs, always counting. In fact, I am hungry, but I save my appetite for my favorite things. I love the bread and roll selection here and always eat more than I should. Then I can never decide between the pâté de foie gras and the lobster bisque for first, so why not have both? Then I will not be too full for something chocolate and delicious for dessert."

"*Oy*," moaned Mitzi, who was always watching her figure and eating sensibly. "Does that come with Maalox or Gelusil?"

"Give me the Maalox now," whispered Betty. "Here comes that repulsive Mrs. Logan Bainbridge, dressed like a tart with her latest gorgeous polo player. How can he look at her? Doesn't she know that those white fish-belly arms are disgusting? And who wants to look at a crepey old *décolleté*? Doesn't she *see* herself?"

"Evidently not, or maybe she just doesn't care," suggested Faith. "Maybe she *likes* dressing as if her skin were as smooth and firm as she remembers it. Maybe it makes her happier than we are?"

"Yes, maybe, but what about the mottled legs? Look at them with the dress slit up to you-know-where!"

"Girls, girls, you are looking at the wrong part of the picture," said Babs, analyzing the assets. "Look, my loves, at the *jewelry*. That is a million-dollar sapphire, for sure. And I bet she just wears it to match blue dresses. The diamond earrings and bracelet, another million, at least, and these are just her little baubles for an early Thursday night dinner. Darlings, she is filthy rich, and her little polo player may be rolling her in the hay, but have no doubt, he's rolling her for her money."

"So how does he do it? Does he have a grandmother fantasy?" giggled Dottie.

"Or maybe he just doesn't wear his contacts when he is out with her—you know, so he sees her kind of blurry, like she once was. I mean, take off your glasses—you can tell she was once a beauty."

They all looked at her, but they got embarrassed as she felt their attention and looked their way. She thought she was being admired, so she preened a bit. Her boyfriend took her hand.

"Yes, but how does he *do* it?"

"Viagra, honey! What do you think?" exclaimed Betty.

"But he is so *young*, is that good for him?"

"As good as it is for the old codgers our age," said Faith. "Who read the article in the *Times* celebrating the fifth anniversary of Viagra?"

"I did," they all chimed in.

"My favorite part was the interview with the doctor in Miami Beach. He was the one who talked about his geriatric patients all clamoring for it. Then he said they get home rarin' to go, but their wives are really not interested. I think this is an exact quote, 'They are all dressed up with nowhere to go,'" said Flossy, leering. And they all laughed at the image in their minds.

"That's the benefit of dating merry widows," concluded Mitzi. "*We* are still interested, right, girls?"

Betty, still working on her champagne, nodded vigorously. "You betcha."

Dottie, who was the only one of them seeing a man regularly, assented, but told them, without wanting to denigrate Sy in their eyes, that there was much, much more to a relationship than sex. They all got the message, and it did not denigrate Sy at all.

"So what do we miss the most?" asked Flossy.

"A summer night on the porch with a light, warm breeze, watching a baseball game while I played solitaire and he caught up on the papers," said Babs.

"Traveling around the world to all the places I ever dreamed of and feeling secure because we were together," said Mitzi.

"*Kvelling* over our grandchildren and telling the same stories over and over again that we could only tell each other. The rest of you would've been bored silly," said Gladys.

"Going to a double feature and dinner at a joint in Chinatown in the days when we had no money," said Faith.

"The rare nights we did not go out," said Dottie.

"Saying good-bye to him every morning he went to work," quipped Betty.

"What about you, Flossy?"

She was silent for a moment as she looked around the room. "I loved coming here with Norman, just the two of us. I also loved coming with our family when they would come to visit. Zoë and Michael would get their little boys all dressed up in their blue blazers and gray slacks, and they would look so beautiful. Norman and I were so proud.

"But there is more, so much more that I miss...everything that you all said, except you, Betty. I wish you'd had some good times when Mel was alive. I bet you did, you just don't want to admit it," she teased.

Betty glowered, and Flossy immediately regretted her comment. Maybe Betty just never cared about Mel and never had the guts to leave him.

So Flossy didn't say what she was really thinking, that she ached for those moments in the middle of the night when she could just reach over and touch Norman and feel him breathing and know she was safe. Now, whenever she awoke with a stab of fear or a shudder of anxiety, she had to comfort herself. It would never, ever be the same. She felt her eyes welling with tears, and to cover up she raised her glass and toasted, "To Michel Canard D'Argent, our man of the moment!"

He was helping to serve their desserts himself, and he relished their accolades. He presented Gladys's dessert last, a huge array of luscious little petits fours with one tiny sparkler in the middle. She had very firmly asked for no fuss, and this was just right. He embraced Gladys and told her she had never looked more beautiful. And at that moment, caught in the candlelight, truly feeling loved by her friends and admired by Monsieur D'Argent, she felt beautiful. The girls all blew kisses and toasted the future and many, many more birthdays.

"Who's treating us next?"

Betty, who was in her cups by now, volunteered, "ME! My birthday is next, and I want to take you all out on the gambling boat for a night!"

"That is so generous, Betty. So are you going to give us gambling money too?"

"Not so fast, sweetie." She wagged her finger at Faith. "I haven't had that much to drink and I'm serious. I've been wanting to go and it would be no fun by myself, and even Babs with her addiction to cards has turned me down. But if I invite you *all*, please say you will do it for my birthday," she begged.

"We accept!"

"And for my birthday, we will go to Miami!"

"And for mine, let's all go on a real cruise!"

"And for mine, let's all go to Paris!" said Flossy.

"Let's go to Tahiti…"

"Let's go to…"

As they all toasted to bigger and bigger ideas, she felt herself enveloped in a heavy black cloud. She could hardly smile anymore, but gamely tried. She couldn't afford any of this. But of course she got carried away when they were all together, as she did tonight. Flossy noticed and asked, "Are you okay?"

"Of course," she said, patting Flossy's arm. "I am just missing my youth. I used to make plans then too…"

CHAPTER TWENTY-THREE

"Jake was dying. His wife sat at the bedside. He looked up and said weakly, 'I have something to confess.'

"'There is no need to,' his wife replied.

"'No,' he insisted. 'I want to die in peace. I slept with your sister, your best friend, her best friend, and your mother!'

"'I know,' she replied. 'Now just rest and let the poison do its work.'"

She laughed out loud as she drove herself home, recalling the joke about a sister in crime. Hers was hardly a crime of vengeance or of passion—no Shakespearean tragedian, she. Hers was a crime of, well, what would she call it? Obvious. Her poisonings were crimes of *necessity.* In order to keep up in Palm Beach, in order to have what she *needed*, in order to *be happy*, she needed more cash. Simple.

Flossy had seen her old self coming through at the end of dinner…just for a moment. A psychiatrist had told her long ago that she would never lose her insecurities and fears completely. Even after years of therapy, he had advised, they would still rise up from time to time, but when it happened, she would know them for what they were and know how to deal with them. Well, for a moment there, she did not. She was overwhelmed with jealousy and self-pity, thinking she could never afford to join in all the plans the girls were making, resenting that she was just not in their league. And Flossy had caught it. What a great reader of body language Flossy was! She would have to stay even more vigilant when Flossy was around. Most of the other girls were pretty oblivious to anything but their own feelings and points of view, but what made Flossy unique among them was her empathy. It was a wonderful quality, of course, but it was dangerous as well. She would have to be on guard always, even against her favorite friend.

And as much as she adored Flossy, she was, admittedly, jealous of her; always had been. She was a hard woman to hate, though, because she was so damn considerate on the one hand and so much fun to be with on the other. But boy, what she would've done for Flossy's life, even today, living with Frances. She even coveted Flossy's memories: the handsome, urbane husband, the beautiful children and grandchildren, her style and energy, her world travels, her fulfillment. She knew Flossy was still hoping she could be independent once again, throw away the oxygen and drive and travel, but considering she almost *died* less than a year ago, she was doing so well. The mysterious lung infection that almost killed her had left her weaker and in need of oxygen when she slept, but other than that she was living a pretty good life. And Frances was scarcely a hardship. Flossy could *afford* her. Which is more than she could say for herself. What would happen if she fell ill?

She could not imagine living with her children, as dutiful as they were. They had no interest in bridge or golf or Palm Beach or shopping, even at The Flea. In fact, they had no interest in money at all. She admired their social service careers, but their houses were small and cramped, they went camping in the Rockies instead of renting houses in Europe like her friends' children, they drove hybrid cars, recycled everything, and spent their money on Birkenstock sandals. When she gave her daughter a gift certificate to a spa for her birthday, she had thanked her, but was horrified at the cost of a pedicure. She thought they loved her but wondered if they liked her. Sometimes they acted a bit condescending of her superficial interests. One had said the other day, "You and your friends are like nuclear reactors that never quite fired up." *What did that mean? That we were full of potential energy but never fulfilled our promise? Or worse, that we could explode at any minute and poison the atmosphere? How ironic*, she thought—*I exploded all right, but I only poisoned two people. I am just a tiny, tiny little reactor.* And perhaps this had been her potential all along. Not what her child had in mind. *Neither my children nor my husband would ever have thought I had the ingenuity, the creativity, the guts, to do what I did…ha ha…good old suburban Mom!*

She thought about her children's attitudes for a while and resolved again to stop feeling insecure. "They love me," she declared out loud. She had worked hard at being a good mother. They knew it and appreciated her for it. She just could not imagine being dependent on them.

But what then? A nursing home? She would rather die. Perhaps she should work on her own demise rather than her friends'. Could she make it as swift and painless as she had done for them? She didn't see why not. In fact, she should have a contingency plan, just in case she got caught. Not that she would ever get caught. There were a few moments of anxiety being interviewed by that handsome Detective Gonzales. But she was sure her anxiety had seemed normal, considering the situation, and everyone considered Bunny's and Paula's deaths accidental. The police had worse things to focus on than the deaths of eighty-five-year-old women. And it was not as if they had suffered. Well, maybe Bunny had—but just for five or ten minutes. She would take that end, but unfortunately she had no fatal allergies. She would have to start amassing some pills…swallow them down and then night-night. Case closed.

But the case was not quite closed. What would be her next move? She could not keep killing off her friends; she would have no one to spend the money with. BUT, they *were all going to die anyway* in the near future. If she was the last, she would try to save up as much as she could, sell the apartment, and book a round-the-world cruise for her swan song. She would love that—the South Seas, Thailand, India, Madagascar, Yawning and already dreaming, she went off to bed.

No brilliant ideas yet, but she was feeling confident a new opportunity would present itself soon.

CHAPTER TWENTY-FOUR

"I didn't attend the funeral, but I sent a nice letter saying I approved of it."

— Mark Twain

Max and Sy were among the pallbearers at Marty's funeral. They were not his good friends, as, sadly, he really didn't have any. In the aftermath of his sudden death, however, they were feeling regrets—regrets that they had not been more understanding, or kinder. After all, they had all known each other since their first years in Palm Beach…those glorious days when they had all been in their early sixties, so excited to have "arrived," to be a part of the beautiful society—the days when they were not yet worried about health and security. Those days had truly been golden and the most carefree of their lives.

"You know, he wasn't such a bad guy," murmured Max almost to himself.

But Sy picked up, as he still had great hearing, and replied, "No, he wasn't such a bad guy, he just had no empathy, and that, at our age, is essential. And especially in his business. He had no sense of timing. He just barged in ten minutes after the funeral and tried to get an exclusive on the dead man's apartment. For Christ's sake, the bodies were hardly cold!

"Forgive me, Marty." He smiled ruefully at the coffin.

"But you know, Sy, he was probably hurting for money. He played the role of *bon vivant*, but I'm guessing he had high blood pressure for good reason. He told us he went into real estate because he was bored, but I'll bet you it was because he needed the cash. Remember, he had a big falling out with his brother, who was the majority owner of their business."

"You're right, you're right, Maxie." They carried the coffin out of the funeral home to the waiting hearse, and they walked off together with their arms flung over each other's shoulders. They agreed that they had spent entirely too much time at this place of late as they headed off for a round of golf. For it was clear to them both—no one needed to say it—that each time they came to this place, they were glad, they were more than glad, they were eternally grateful that they were still the mourners, not the poor fellow in the coffin.

"Did you hear the one about the mortician working late one night?"

"Tell me, tell me, I always like a great funeral joke," cackled Sy.

"Well, he examined the body of Mr. Schwartz, who was about to be cremated, and he made a startling discovery. Schwartz had the largest private part he had ever seen.

"'I'm sorry, Mr. Schwartz,' the mortician said to the dead body, 'I can't allow you to be cremated with such an impressive private part. It must be saved for posterity.'

"So he removed it, stuffed it into his briefcase, and took it home. 'I have something to show you that you won't believe,' he said to his wife as he opened his briefcase

"'My God!' his wife exclaimed. 'Schwartz is dead!'"

"Schwartz is dead, Schwartz is dead…wishful thinking that *your* parts will be saved," whispered Betty, who had been walking out to the parking lot just beside them. "You are only hoping you will be recognized too!"

"Betty, my love," ogled Max, "just give me the chance."

"You had your chance long ago, Maxie, when you still had your real hair. Too late now!"

Self-consciously, Max reached up and adjusted his toupee as he shuffled off with Sy. "Speaking of empathy, there's a woman who has not a whit!"

"Maxie, you take her too seriously. That's her idea of flirting. She is so bad at it, she never gets a date. No wonder poor Mel died young!"

They had a good laugh and drove off while Betty joined the rest of the girls. "So, darlings, are we going to celebrate this occasion by going out to lunch?"

"God, Betty, you are on a roll of foot-in-mouth. Find a little kindness down deep. I know it is there," said Mitzi, pretending to peer into Betty's blouse.

"Ah, Mitzi, I need to take sweetness-and-light lessons from you. Maybe you can teach me how to get a man."

"Hey, y'all, I am going to drive with Betty and teach her some southern etiquette. We'll meet you at the club." Mitzi wrapped her pink chiffon scarf around Betty's neck and teased her out of her sour mood.

Babs, who was driving Flossy, couldn't get over Betty's mood. "Do you think she forgets her meds or something? Or maybe it's because she needs a drink? What's with her these days? She just seems to be getting worse and worse."

"I don't know," sighed Flossy. "I think that we all are dealing with getting older, with being the next person in the coffin (she shuddered as she said this) in different ways."

"And you're saying that you think Betty deals by being angry and nasty?"

"Sure, it gets out her anxiety, without having to deal with the real source…you know that."

"I suppose you are right, but she's going to lose her friends if she keeps this up, and that will make matters so much worse."

"No, I don't think so. We have so much water under the bridge together, we're used to each other's foibles, and we feel comfortable with each other."

"You're probably right, Floss, but I don't know. If we have so little time left, I mean even if we are lucky and get *ten* more years, don't we want to make every moment count? I find I have so much less tolerance than I used to. I only have time for the good stuff now. If we are lucky as we are, we don't have to worry about money or our kids or even our relationships with our husbands. We only have to take care of *us*!"

"Oh, I don't know that it is that simple, Babsie. I still worry about my kids, and they are adults with families of their own. But still, when one of them has a setback, I feel it as if they were twelve years old. I think I will always worry about my kids. Don't you? Or am I just being an old Jewish grandmother?"

"Flossy, you *are* an old Jewish *great*-grandmother. There is no getting around that!"

When they arrived at the club, the valet took Babs's car, and they strolled through the entrance arbor laden with pink clematis and exotic orchids. The golf course beyond was lush with palm and citrus trees lining the fairways. The fragrance of tropical plants filled the air, and as Flossy and Babs took in their surroundings, they breathed deeply, and for the moment, they felt content.

Greeting friends as they table-hopped through the glass-enclosed dining room, they joined the girls' table. And coincidentally, they walked into a continuation of their discussion. Dottie was passing around a piece of paper. "You won't believe what I found in my husband's drawer. I was looking for a tie for Sy, as we had decided to go to Chez Jean Pierre for a bite, and he wasn't comfortable without a tie, and I knew I had some old ones around for the kids to wear when they come. You know kids never wear ties anymore—I don't think my sons even *own* them."

"You found a pair of silk panties," hooted Gladys, knowing very well this was not the case, as Dottie's husband, Richard, had not been the type to philander.

"Ha ha…hardly. But what I did find was just as upsetting. Look at this. It's a poem, sort of free verse, written by my daughter, about her *father.* I don't know if she gave it to him and he never showed it to me, or if she wrote it after he died and stuck it in his bureau as a message or something. Read this!" She sniffed while she looked for some Kleenex.

Gladys handed her a tissue while she read out loud:

Third Quarter

Written on a Thanksgiving Weekend

This morning my friend John came to do some carpentry work. He kept his radio turned up high, and it delivered the sounds of a football game into my world. In fifty years, that droning singsong hasn't changed at all, has it?

Today, with the full moon jamming my circuits open, my armor all in disarray…I became a little girl again, back in Larchmont:

"Oh, the game is on! That means Daddy will be on the couch, listening to the TV and reading the newspaper…I'll bring him some pretzels and ginger ale. And cheer when he cheers."

That's the closest I could ever get to you, Richard. Waiting, like a lab retriever, for the stick that you never threw.

Now, I don't read newspapers much, don't have a television, don't drink soda or eat pretzels,

I'm past the half-time now, well into the third quarter. And yet, this child is still waiting, somewhere, motionless, for Richard to say something kind or hopeful or affectionate.

You sit here with me, little one. We'll watch the moon together and you can know by the three tears on my cheek that someone really loves you.

"*Oh my God,* that is so poignant," cried Faith, huge tears welling in her eyes.

Most of the girls were feeling dampish while Dottie just sobbed miserably. "Who would have thought she felt so left out by him? I thought we gave her *everything.* He never liked kids much, I guess, but his own *daughter*—this is how he made her feel…as a grown woman. I can't bear it. How could I have been so oblivious? How could *he*?" She dissolved again.

Sy, seeing Dottie crying from across the room, rushed over and pulled her up into his arms. Grateful for his comfort and concern, she let him walk her away while she told him the story. She thought, *How different he is from Richard, who, honestly, would have tossed the note away as overblown teenage angst. Did he ever know? Would he have cared at all? And now I can never make it right.* She leaned into Sy's chest and felt consoled, but miserable.

The girls were unusually quiet, each lost in her own reverie of the past, wondering what they did not see or feel or know about their children's unhappiness or husbands' dissatisfactions or, for that matter, acknowledge as their own.

CHAPTER TWENTY-FIVE

Frances was driving Flossy to the bridge game the next day, and they started chattering, as they often did now, about Roberto.

"I am so glad to be your romantic confidante and advisor," declared Flossy. "Your relationship with Roberto is so full of optimism and excitement. It is so hopeful for me. It's so much cheerier than who's sick and who has died, whose children are in trouble, and it's so much more consequential than who has insulted whom and who bid four spades when she should've passed. I love my friends, but I must admit our conversations are most often either sad or superficial.

"I hope for sparkle from my kids, but honestly, most of the time they are too busy. On the phone they breeze through how everything is fine and say they've got to go. It's as if they stride through life being decisive and strong, solving their problems and those of their kids, even telling *me* what to do.

"And yet," Flossy prattled on in a different vein, "when they get down here, they let down their guard and become children again. Everything pours out. I think being with me *allows* them to feel more vulnerable, you know? In some ways, I am still Mommy—certainly when things go wrong. I know just by their telling me they feel better. Frankly, I don't have to say much more than, 'I understand.' Poor Zoë comes down here so exhausted from trying to do everything so perfectly—work, wife, mother, God knows what else—that she sometimes just cries and cries. Then she picks herself up, washes her face, gives me a big hug, and says, 'Thanks, Mom, I needed that.' Then I remind her of my favorite solution when things get overwhelming. I tell her to go into her closet, take down her biggest pocketbook—you and I know Zoë only has one—open it up, stick her head in, and scream. Then she is to close the pocketbook, put it back on the shelf, and walk back into the room, and she will feel much better. The trick worked for me for many years. I would do it now, but you would hear me and come running in!"

Flossy sighed. "I guess no matter how grown up or successful one gets, everyone would like a mother's reassurance from time to time. Even Michael, as much as he is a grown man, lets down his guard and allows himself to be needy with me, and I've tried to keep that door open for my grandsons too. You know they used to share their dating problems with me? Their old grandmother was somehow safer than their own parents. Why the other day..."

Frances could not help chuckling at Flossy's pocketbook solution, but for the most part she had been quietly listening to Flossy go on and on about being a mother to her grown children and grandchildren. Unused to Frances not chattering back to her, Flossy looked at her quizzically and then blurted out her realization.

"Oh my God, Frances, how could I be so insensitive? You have never had a mother who you could cry to...I am so sorry."

"It's okay, Mrs. Kane," Frances replied rather formally. She did not much want to continue her conversation about Roberto.

"Frances, Frances, Frances, don't stay angry at me. I was acting like a meandering-minded old lady. I started by saying how interested I am in your life, and I mean it. You are much, much more than a caretaker to me. I love you...you know that. I am so sorry to hurt you. And because I love you, I'm so happy that you have Roberto. We are not mother and daughter, we are…we are once-in-a-lifetime friends! And besides, this is how we can reverse roles; I get to take care of you."

"I like that, Flossita, 'once-in-a-lifetime' friends. And I forgive you because you would forgive me, I know, and I know you are, well, not a totally perfect person."

"I'm not? I always knew I wasn't a perfect *patient*, but I always thought I was quite perfect as a person," Flossy teased.

"Not a perfect person, Flossita, but a perfect friend."

While Frances put her foot on the brake, they leaned against their seat belts and embraced, while the horns honked behind them on South Ocean Boulevard. "Oops, and I am driving like a meandering-minded native," laughed Frances.

And Flossy continued where they left off, "So what more have you found out about Roberto?"

"You know, Flossy, I know a lot about how he feels about things, about what I would call his *corazon*, his solid noble center, his decency, and his deep, deep empathy for other people, not only innocent victims of senseless crime, but for you—excuse me for saying this, but for older people in general, and for *me*. It is because of his special sensibility toward older people, I think, that he *likes* being in Palm Beach. He likes helping…

"But I still know very little about his past. He's not yet ready to tell me, but there is *something* there, I know it. He grew up and went to college in Miami is all I know."

"What about his family?"

"Not sure. I know he has an older sister in Miami, and I know his parents are alive, but I get the feeling he does not see them much, if at all.

"And of course I am *dying* to know about his past girlfriends, about why he never married. I know he has had lots of girlfriends because when we meet his friends they all allude to it, but his lips are sealed. Any time I go near the subject, he makes a U-turn."

"Whatever you do, don't press him. He will tell you when he can. The worst thing you can do right now is try to pry him open against his will. I'll bet you that one of the things he loves about you most is that he doesn't *have* to deal with those ghosts or skeletons or whatever they are when he is with you. He loves that you distract him from dark memories. So bite your tongue. I know you want to know, but timing is everything, my little Francesca."

"Hey, Flossita, that's what he says too! So I am listening to my two best friends."

With exaggerated air kisses and a smile, Frances waved Flossy off into Babs's building for the afternoon game.

The girls had picked up where they left off on the subject of Dottie's daughter. Dottie was still so distraught that she couldn't concentrate on the cards.

"Enough of this!" said Flossy, slamming her hand down on the table and stopping the play. "I want you to call her right now!"

"Now? Here?"

"Absolutely. Go into the kitchen and have some privacy. With the time difference between here and Los Angeles, it's likely you'll find her at home because it's still pretty early morning there. Get it off your chest, and let her get it off hers. *Imagining* her feelings is always much, much worse that talking about them. Go."

Dottie obeyed orders and trotted off to the kitchen. Babs, counting as usual, muttered, "I hope she is going to use her credit card. This could be an expensive call."

"For God's sake, Babs, Flossy is right," said Faith, rolling her eyes at the others. "Have a little generosity. You can afford a fifteen-dollar phone call."

"I know, but all the same, I'm going in there to check." She tiptoed into the kitchen and, having seen Dottie's credit card on the counter, announced to the group that the call was on Dottie's nickel, and scribbling on a pad, she scored the last hand.

As Gladys took her turn shuffling, she asked, "Did anyone hear that piece on NPR this morning about how young people today are feeling so alone?"

"*Oy veh*, I did," said Faith. "I read the original article in the *Atlantic* last month. And this is even when they're married, have friends and kids and jobs! It's that they are *so* busy and working *so* hard they don't have time to talk to each other. It's sad."

"Oh, I don't know how different it is from our day," said Mitzi. "We *chose* not to tell…so much was left unsaid. We just kept our feelings bottled up inside, such stereotypical nineteen-fifties housewives with frilly aprons and smiling faces. And our husbands, they surely didn't confide in each other, they just went off and played golf and guffawed at each other's puerile jokes."

"Hey, wait a minute, Mitzi, you've been married three times, you must have had some intimate, confiding moments."

"I was a good listener and supporter, but honestly, we didn't talk about deep insecurities or desperate feelings."

"And now everyone wants to talk about everything—but they don't have the time," summarized Betty. "Well, my new, sweeter self wants to tell you all that I'm happy that we have *time* together and that we can trust each other to talk about anything. Well, *almost* anything."

Babs winked almost imperceptibly at Flossy, acknowledging their conversation of the day before, that Betty would truly stay one of them, despite her foibles.

At that moment, Dottie emerged from the kitchen, tucking away her credit card and searching as usual for a tissue. "Oh, Floss, you were so right to encourage me to call," she acknowledged. "My daughter said that I was never meant to find the note, that she had written it after Richard died, but it was just her way of putting away her childhood. 'Believe me, Mom,' she said, 'far from being sad, this stuff actually unshackles old memories and gives me more energy.' My daughter has a very Zen way of expressing herself." She smiled ruefully. "But I believe her, and we had a wonderful conversation. She's coming down in a few weeks to visit." Dottie glowed.

"That's terrific, Dot…warms the cockles of my heart," exclaimed Betty, quickly reverting to her old sassy self. "But does that mean you'll miss my birthday party on the gambling boat?"

"Not for a million dollars, Betty-sweet…well, maybe a million, but I already told Sy I could not go to the United Way gala with him that night, so you know where my priority is."

"*Wow*!" they all said at once, as they knew this was a big deal for Dottie.

"Gee, I'll go with him," teased Gladys. "Not that I am trying to steal Sy, but you know, I might be able to meet someone."

"No, no, no, honey," admonished Betty. "You are coming with me."

As they were about to leave, Dottie thanked Flossy again for insisting that she call her daughter, and Flossy related her dream of the night before. "I dreamt of Zoë and can't quite remember what is was about, but I woke up and felt as if I had had a revelation…that Zoë had grown up and she would be okay. I immediately called her to tell her, and she shook my seriousness aside and laughed. 'Mom,' she said, 'I am *sixty-two* years old.' I don't think she yet understands how we never stop worrying. It's in our DNA."

As they all drove off, she contemplated her friends fondly, yet with an air of condescension. How were they still so attached to their pasts? Was it their way of fighting the future? Of not facing the inevitable that stared them in the mirror every day? Well, not her. She was taking control of the future until her very last breath, ha ha…or dollar. And speaking of which, where was the next tranche of dollars to come from? She still had no plan, but she had many considerations. Perhaps she should have been holding her nose and courting Marty. Not that he had any significant money; they all realized that quickly enough. But he did have credit cards she could have utilized, and with his high blood pressure he would have been an easy one to knock off. Oh well, spilt milk and all that. She would have to look for another opportunity. Of course there was Max, but she did not think she could bear him. He was smart, but just too ridiculous. And that one that Mitzi dumped so quickly—he might be a candidate…he was dumb enough to believe anything. Perhaps she would look into him. What was his name? And how could she manage to bump into him?

She drove off to The Flea. She had won big that afternoon—$20.00—and she was determined to spend it. Would that she could afford Worth Avenue…

CHAPTER TWENTY-SIX

"He is not only dull himself, he is the cause of dullness in others."
— Samuel Johnson

Lost in reverie, she strolled around The Flea, not really looking at anything, just passing time and taking comfort in the process. There wasn't much here she had not already bought.

Absentmindedly she rummaged through some cheap silk scarves, meant to be Pucci or Hermes but obviously knockoffs. Now that she had developed the taste for the *real thing*—the clothes she bought with Bunny's credit card, then the lingerie, then those beautiful sheets—she didn't get much of a thrill from the phony look-alikes here at The Flea. Her own psyche had let her down; she surmised she couldn't go back again, but where could she go?

Tossing the scarves back in their bin, she turned and walked right into an elderly man.

"Uh, hi. What are *you* doing here?" she asked by way of introduction. Catching herself, as she did not mean to be rude, she continued, "I'm sorry, I didn't mean to bump into you, nor start out with such a blunt question, but aren't you Sy's friend from Boca?"

"Don't be sorry, I'm delighted to meet someone I know. You are one of the girls, right? And I am Sam Rabin." He offered his hand.

She introduced herself as well, and they made small talk as they walked up and down the aisles together. "So, if I may ask more politely, what *are* you doing here? Are you looking for something special or just browsing about like me?"

"Actually, I'm looking for something to add to my collection," confided Sam.

"Your collection? What could you be collecting that you might find here?"

"Ah, I'd have to know you a little better to tell. It's something so dear to me, you'd have to see it to believe it."

Good grief, she thought. *This is getting either interesting or creepy. I hope it isn't ladies' underwear or something.* But aloud she said with a smile, "Well, that sounds intriguing!"

"Well, to me it is. But how about you? What is a gorgeous, well-dressed gal like you doing here?"

"Oh, just passing the time. Many years ago I used to be involved in the fashion industry," she lied, "and I am always interested in seeing how Worth Avenue is copied here—you know, the almost Ralph Laurens, the practically Emilio Puccis…stuff like that."

"Well, you belong on Worth Avenue is all I can say." He smiled appreciatively at her. "How about we go have a drink at Taboo?"

"Delighted—you have certainly figured out where to see and be seen since you moved here." And what she thought was, *He can't be* that *stupid—he knows the right place to go for a drink at five o'clock.*

They chatted about his moving, his new apartment, his attempt to decorate it, his children, and his golf. He was fine at the small talk, although after an hour it was running low, and he never asked a question, until—"How about we go for a walk down the street? Maybe we can find a real Ralph Lauren for you!"

She coyly demurred at the gift offer, but she agreed to the walk. So they strolled past all the glittering windows on Worth Avenue, in and out of bougainvillea-draped alleys, admiring the clothes and jewelry, the Louis XIV furniture, the gargantuan homes pictured in the realty windows. It turned out that Sam was quite a clotheshorse, and as she really looked at him for the first time, she realized he was not unattractive—at least for a man his age. He kept himself well—his face was close-shaven and his hair, which was scant, was nevertheless elegantly cut. He told her his favorite store was Trillion, aptly named for its wildly expensive but beautifully tailored sportswear. She was sure his sweater of thin azure cashmere came from there. In fact, as they passed by, the owner waved at Sam like an old friend. She knew that a simple cashmere crewneck from Trillion cost at least $1,000 and surmised that Sam might be the answer to her prayers.

Sam asked her to have dinner, but playing it cool, she turned him down, saying she had to get back to her car as she had a dinner date. He seemed overjoyed when she said she would be happy to see him again.

And she did. She began "seeing" Sam three to four times a week. He was lonely, and with just a little effort, he was easy to please. As was often the case with boring people, he rarely asked about her, so all she had to do was ask a question, and he was off and yammering about nothing. A simple "How are you?" resulted in at least a half-hour description of that day's aches and pains. "How was your golf today?" resulted in a hole-by-hole description of every shot from drive to putt.

This night he had spent almost the entire meal on his golf game. "And then I missed my first sand shot, so I took another try and sprayed the sand all over, and the ball landed on the *other* side of the green in another sand trap, and..."

Well, at least he hasn't got Alzheimer's, she consoled herself as she dug into her brand-new Gucci bag, courtesy of Sam. By the time he got to the eighteenth hole, she had powdered her nose with her new Chanel compact and admired her new Cartier earrings in the mirror, thanks to Sam. They were just finishing dinner at the ever-so-expensive and chic Café Boulud, and she was content to relish the atmosphere and the food, if not the company.

She knew the girls would wonder how she could do it, but they weren't at Boulud, were they? They were home alone or playing yet another tedious game of bridge. She wondered, not for the first time, what the rest of her life would be like with Sam—having everything she ever wanted in life: clothes, jewelry, travel, chauffeured cars, and even private planes. He had already told her that when he went to St. Barths with his late wife, they flew commercial to Puerto Rico but then chartered a plane for themselves from there, as they couldn't bear the crowds at the St. Maarten airport. He told her of sailing yachts they had chartered in the Mediterranean, of shopping at Akris and Armani (he knew all the names), of golfing from Santa Barbara to New Zealand...hole by hole. She sighed, coveting it all and wondering if his wife had been bored to death.

So she tried. "So what do you think of the upcoming election? Did you read Tom Friedman in the *Times* this morning?"

Silence. Was it possible he did not know who Tom Friedman was?

So she pushed a little. "He wrote a wonderful piece about how the Democrats need to be clearer about what they have accomplished in the last four years."

His eyes glazed over.

Uh-oh, she thought. "Dare I ask, are you a Republican?"

"I don't follow politics too closely. I'm an issue-based voter."

That sounded promising, so she asked, of course, "And what are the issues that are most important to you?"

"Not issues, just one—taxes—I don't like to pay them!"

"So you *are* a Republican," she pronounced. "I would love to discuss our differences of opinion."

"No, no, no, I can't do that—I am nothing."

"As I feared," she muttered.

"My dear, let's change the subject. What do you think of coming home with me for a nightcap? I think we have spent enough time together for me to show you my collection. I just had the display cases finished, and I am *ready.*" He squeezed her arm in anticipation.

She managed a wan smile and hoped for the best.

CHAPTER TWENTY-SEVEN

Riding back to Sam's apartment, she was filled with happiness.

Sam had tipped handsomely—she liked generosity in a man. He had walked her around to the passenger side of his sleek little Mercedes convertible and graciously held the door open for her. He considerately asked her if she would like the top down or if it would muss her hair.

"Oh, Sam, if you don't mind me disheveled, I don't," she replied.

As they drove along South Ocean Boulevard under the full moon, she was transfixed by the lights of the beautiful homes that faced the sea and wondered what it would be like to live in one of them, or to have a boat, just a small yacht, tied up at the end of the back lawn that sloped down to the Intracoastal Waterway, to entertain her friends in her garden room with French doors opening onto the terrace, to swim languid laps in her own pool. Holding Sam's hand as he drove, she told herself, *I can* do *this. It's no harder pretending to be interested in his conversation than to murder someone.* She giggled to herself. *And besides, he is quiet now, and we are both relaxed and feel no need to talk. With times like these and eight hours of sleeping and his mornings on the golf course without me, how bad can it be? And I will have ev-er-y-thing!*

She shouted "hooray" to the moon, and Sam was pleased.

His apartment was spacious and airy, furnished in a minimalist style appropriate to a bachelor. The walls were covered with sporting prints, the shelves with his late wife's collection of deco glass. It was quite simply stunning, but there was not a book in sight. Huge glass doors opened onto wide terraces facing east to the Atlantic and west to the Intracoastal Waterway.

"So you see," Sam said with pride, "I have sunrise and sunset, just like the song!"

"The song?"

"You know, from *Fiddler on the Roof.* 'Sunrise, sunset, swiftly flow the days…'"

"Oh, Sam, you've never told me you like the theater. I *adore* the theater. My late husband and I had repertory subscriptions and always got tickets for the best shows on Broadway…"

"Sshhh," he said, holding his finger up to her lips. "I actually like the theater for sleeping in, but I know the song because I danced to it with my daughter at her wedding. She made me practice and practice."

Her heart sank as he crooned, "Sunrise, sunset," waltzing her toward the bedroom wing.

Uh-oh, she thought, and she began to blush with anxiety. *Is he really taking me to bed? Is this like the old line, 'Come see my etchings, my dear,' and there are no etchings?*

At that moment, when she was sure there would be no *collection* of anything, he turned on the lights of the second bedroom and declared, "Voilà!"

And before her eyes she saw it—the collection. Rows and rows and rows of…golf balls. All white golf balls. Hundreds and hundreds of all white golf balls.

"*Wow*, Sam—what a lot of golf balls you have!" she exclaimed, smothering her guffaw. *Well, that was pretty obvious*, she thought. But what else could she say? They're gorgeous? They're *so unusual*?

"You like them?"

"Oh yes, I do—this must be the largest collection around, I mean outside of a pro shop."

"Well, in all modesty, it *is*. It is the second largest in the country, but you see it is not just quantity. Anyone can buy a lot of golf balls. The idea is to get three of each different label or marking, so all of these on the south and north walls are complete sets. Those on the west wall are *in*-complete sets that I am still working on."

"Gee, Sam—that's quite a, quite a, uh—challenge!"

"Oh, I knew you would understand. So that's why I was at The Flea—it is places like that where you can find really unusual sets. You know, balls that did not quite make it in the country club set, so were sold off to bargain places like The Flea. I found one set at a tag sale—now where is it?—imprinted with tiny mosquitoes. Can you imagine?"

He proudly held them as if they were the most delicate of Fabergé eggs and allowed her to touch them. "They are from a rain forest golf course in Costa Rica, and extremely rare, because you see the golf course did not last too long. Too many real mosquitoes, I guess. Ha ha."

"Oh, that must have been *quite a find*, Sam."

"It was, it was…but let me show you these here with little pimples on them, and these with delicate blades of grass, and…"

Sam was gushing over his collection of white golf balls. He explained how he had considered adding balls of different colors but feared they would taint the purity of his collection. He began walking her around the room describing each and every set—what they symbolized, how he found them, and how he decided to work with a very talented craftsman to display them. Stifling yawn after yawn, she figured she would be there until two in the morning, as they had not even finished one half of one wall.

"Sam, I've had such a long day, I can't give this the attention it properly deserves. How about that quick nightcap and then taking me home? I'll come back to see the rest during the day when I can really focus. You've just wined and dined me so extravagantly, I seem to be a little woozy."

"Oh, of course, my dear, let's just have a quick brandy to settle our stomachs, and we'll be off. But you *will* come back so I can share the rest with you, won't you please?"

"Of course I will, Sam," she tried to say without sounding patronizing.

While sipping her brandy she was reminded of a funny golf story. "Sam, you will appreciate this. A college classmate of my husband's became quite well known for having one of the earliest sex change operations. In school this classmate had been a man—and a tremendous athlete. When he became a woman, he did not lose his athletic prowess. The two of them always played money golf together in college, and shortly after the sex change, my husband called his friend and invited him to play golf as they always had done. So they got on the first tee together, and my husband teed off with a nice drive. His friend then started to move the cart to the *ladies'* tee! 'Oh no, my friend,' said my husband, 'just because you now have breasts and a you-know-what does not mean you get that advantage over me—get back here to the men's tee and hit the ball!'

"This is a *true* story, Sam…isn't it a riot?"

Blank stare. "I don't get it."

"Sam, Sam, his friend *used* to be a man. Now his friend is a woman but still has the same athletic ability she had when she was a man, so it wouldn't be fair, would it, if she teed off from the ladies' tee, which would give her a fifty-yard advantage? Don't you think it was a funny comment—'Get back here to the men's tee?'"

"But why would he play with a woman like that?"

"Why wouldn't he play with a woman? Wouldn't you play with me?"

"Yes, of course I would, but you are a woman for real, not a…a trans-trans-whatever woman."

"But they were *friends*—why should it matter?"

Sam looked sheepish. "I don't know, it just does."

It was time to go home. She couldn't have this discussion. She gave him a sisterly kiss goodnight and assured him she would see him again soon, but not tomorrow.

Throwing off her clothes and throwing herself onto her bed, she tried to put off thinking about Sam, but it was impossible. *He* was impossible: impossibly dull, impossibly uninterested in the world, impossibly ignorant. But he was sweet, too sweet to kill, although she sure knew enough about his high blood pressure, his heart problems, and his reflux. *If* she held on long enough, *and* he married her, and *then* he died, she would have all she wanted. But she yelled at the walls, *"I couldn't bear it!"*

The girls at least were funny and smart and worldly. They read the newspaper, they went to the theater, they read *books*. Sam bought clothes and collected golf balls. "*Golf balls...plain white golf balls!* I'd rather be poor."

But he was as nice to her as he knew how to be. He was so grateful for her attention. He thought she was beautiful. When had a man last told her that? And he liked to buy her things. She would have to let him down easy...but what to do for money?

CHAPTER TWENTY-EIGHT

"Que linda, Flossita!"

"You like?" Flossy held out her dress and twirled, but on her high heels she teetered and almost lost her balance.

As Frances reached out to steady her, she acted as if she was just holding Flossy by the arms to get a better view. Flossy knew that Frances saw that she almost fell, but they both carried on as if nothing happened.

"You look beautiful and lucky to me!" exclaimed Frances, giving Flossy her most scrutinizing appraisal. "Hmmmm…" She closed her eyes and swayed, pretending to await inspiration. "My ESP tells me you are going to win $567 tonight!"

"Well, if I do, it's because you willed it, so half of it is yours," Flossy promised.

"*Ai, muchacha*, you don't have to share it with me—you share your whole life with me already," replied Frances while arranging Flossy's light cashmere shawl over her shoulders.

At that moment the doorbell rang, and Frances ran to get it, because Flossy was being picked up tonight by Faith and Babs. She felt comfortable letting Flossy go to Betty's birthday party on the gambling boat with the "responsible" girls. She would never have let her drive with Betty, who she was sure would drink much too much on her birthday. But it was not the girls—it was Roberto.

He gave Frances a quick kiss on her neck, but his eyes were already on Flossy. "You take my breath away, Mrs. Kane. You are beautiful tonight. How old did you say you were? No more than fifty-two, I would say."

As he took her hand, she moved toward him and put her hand on his cheek. Eyeing him provocatively, she replied in her best movie star voice, "You don't look so bad yourself, handsome!" With that, she rose up on her tiptoes to give him a lingering kiss on his cheek and announced, "I'm off to conquer the world, seduce a handsome croupier, and win $567!"

"I believe the first two," nodded Roberto, "but how do you know you will win precisely $567?"

"Because Frances told me I would, and I believe everything she says—even about *you*, you flirtatious man!"

With that, the girls arrived to drive her to the boat, so she batted her eyelashes and sashayed out the door like Loretta Young.

"Whew, that was steamy," said Frances, pretending to fan herself. "If I did not know better, I could be jealous."

"She reminds me of how my grandmother looked when I was a boy...so sexy. I mean, for an older woman. She, my grandmother, had the same elegance, and yet there is nothing old about them. I practiced flirting with my grandmother when I was twelve. She was so safe and sweet, but boy oh boy, she never forgot how to be a woman..."

Roberto looked away for a moment, as if he had to regroup, and Frances gave him his privacy. She knew there was more to the story of his grandmother, but she was patient.

"Come," she said as she led him out to the terrace, "there is a beautiful sunset, and we have the whole night together. Flossy won't be home until midnight at the earliest."

He turned back to her, and throwing his arm over her shoulder, he pulled her close as they walked outside together. "You want to know, don't you?" he asked.

"Only when you are ready to tell me," she said so unaffectedly he knew she really meant it. And he was ready to confide the story that had broken his heart.

Taking a sip of wine, he began. "We were certainly not rich in Cuba—no one we knew was rich—but we were not poor, not really poor, either. My parents just wanted more for us, like most parents do for their families. Castro's Cuba was a dead end. Through people who knew people, they arranged to get my sister and me out to Miami.

"I didn't want to go. I was a happy child, oblivious to politics. I was only interested in baseball and the novels of Ellery Queen. But most of all I cared about my grandmother, who gave me more love than I deserved. It was she who woke me every morning, she who made my breakfast, and she who slicked my hair down, combed it, and sent me off to school. Even when I was no longer a little one, and my pals were hanging outside the door waiting for me, I would not leave until she folded me in her arms to say goodbye. Even when they razzed me, I didn't care. I couldn't imagine starting a new life without this woman who loved me completely. Whatever I did was okay with her.

"But my parents insisted. We argued every night. They promised and swore that they would follow soon after with my grandmother, that they would never leave her alone in Cuba. So I believed them. And I didn't know she was ill.

"My sister and I lived with a cousin for a year before my parents managed to get away. They didn't bring my grandmother. They left her…they left her…alone and sick…to die…alone, without me, in Cuba. They told me she wasn't strong enough to make the journey, and she was being cared for in a nursing home. I kicked and screamed and told them I was going back to be with her. I told them I hated them and that I would never forgive them."

The memory of how he felt that day when his parents turned up on the doorstep in Miami was almost more than he could bear. He had been telling the story resolutely, sitting with his fists clenched, one hand on his hip, his eyes wide open. As his eyes closed and the tears came, he collapsed into Frances's arms and sobbed.

She didn't say, "Sshhhh, it will be all right." She didn't say a word. She just rubbed his back and stroked his hair and let him cry. It would never really be all right, but she knew telling her had been a big step.

"I tried to get back, but can you imagine what a thirteen-year-old boy could do? *Nothing.* How could I get back to Cuba? One day we got a letter saying she had passed away peacefully. Can you imagine what it was like for her in a disgusting nursing home all alone without her family? I imagined it every day for years, and I hated my parents.

"Eventually, and I mean eventually—not until sometime in college—I began to reconcile myself to what had happened, to understand my parents, and to rebuild a civil relationship with them. Today I guess I understand, but I have learned that to understand does not mean to forgive. I think I actually love them, but the barrier will always be there—always.

"So now you know what makes me tick, why I get so much satisfaction out of being a cop in a community of senior citizens who I can help and be there for, always making up for not being there for her."

"Or maybe, just maybe the affection you get from the people here is the only affection you can really trust."

"No, no, my Francesca, that is not true. I would not have told you if I did not see in those deep brown eyes that you were the best woman I have ever known."

She pulled away from him a bit and the words spilled out, "Maybe, just maybe you have never allowed yourself to have a permanent relationship because you are afraid of losing it the way you lost the first male-female relationship you ever had with your *abuela*. Maybe I am just another of a long string of women who you have seduced and..."

As the words tumbled out, she could not believe how stupid she had been. Roberto jumped up and looked at her in shock. How could she…just when he had shared the emotions he hardly ever let himself feel or, for that matter, even acknowledged to himself?

At that moment his beeper went off, preventing him from saying the hurtful things he was thinking. "Gotta go," he said. "It's the station." It *was* the station, but there was no emergency, just the sergeant checking his communications network, but Roberto knew he had to go. He needed to think about what had just happened. He needed to understand why. Was she so insecure in his love? Was it his fault? He had to *think*. Without a word, he walked out the door.

Frances cried and cried, and no one rubbed her back or stroked her hair.

CHAPTER TWENTY-NINE

"A nice Jewish boy who was working in the family business knew that he was going to inherit a fortune when his sickly father died. One night at a party, he saw the most beautiful woman he'd ever seen. Her beauty took his breath away, so he walked over to her and said, 'I might look like an ordinary guy, but in a few months, my father will die and I'll inherit sixty million dollars.' The woman was impressed and took his business card. A week later, she became his stepmother.

"The motto: women are so much better at estate planning than men."

The girls laughed grimly at the joke, because it was much too late for them to do this kind of estate planning. They were the old ones now, and they could be sickly at any moment. They wondered if the fawning young croupiers who were so overly effusive were hoping to be remembered in their wills.

"I am *not* kidding," exclaimed Mitzi, tossing her chiffon scarf. "That cute one over there asked me what I am doing when I get off the boat tonight! *Moi!* I am sure he is after my money, and he thinks I am just a dumb old lady to be exploited." She pulled her pocketbook in toward her chest.

"Come on, Mitzi, I can't believe I am telling you, of all people, to just enjoy the flirtation," advised Dottie.

"He is just much too young and *virile*," protested Mitzi. "And besides, *I'm* used to being the aggressive one, but with men my own age, who I *know* appreciate my charms," she said as she turned down her lips into what she perceived as a provocative little moue. "Although they may not be able to *do* anything about it, at least it's fun. That guy is intimidating."

"No one is making a pass at me," cried Gladys piteously.

"Oh, sweetie, no one is making a pass at me, either," comforted Flossy, putting her arm around Gladys. "No one is making a pass at any of us. We are just supposed to be enjoying the game and making a little money on the side."

"What do *you* need the money for?" demanded Betty. "You don't need it. Leave some on the table for the rest of us. Are you going to walk off with all the winnings, *as usual*? How do you win here anyway? Give the croupier a sip of your oxygen?"

Faith told Betty to behave, and Flossy ignored her, smug in the fact that she was, in fact, winning.

"Well, I think it's smart to be cautious. I just can't keep throwing my money on the tables. I feel like George Washington's Jewish mother—do you know this one?" giggled Babs. "'Next time I catch you throwing money across the Potomac, you can kiss your allowance good-bye!'"

Peals of laughter ensued, and Betty was the loudest of them all. She had treated them to a gigantic buffet dinner, which offered twice as much as any of them could eat, and the wine and liquor were flowing. Betty seemed to think the free drinks were in honor of her birthday and graciously accepted one every five minutes. The rest, as usual, tried to be temperate. But the champagne circulating around the room went down very easily, and it was hard for them to monitor how much they were drinking as they moved from blackjack to roulette to the slots, and freshly filled glasses magically appeared at their sides. So they were all a bit tipsy, but only Betty appeared to be rocking back and forth to the rhythm of the sea.

They all seemed to be spending freely—even Babs, with her counting, and Dottie, who said she was thinking of all her favorite charities—but no one was spending more than Betty.

"So here's where you made your killing, Flossy," said Betty as she stumbled over to the blackjack table where the chips were stacked in front of Flossy. "This must be a lucky table." Betty plopped herself down and began to bet foolishly and, of course, continued to lose. Ogling the croupier lasciviously, she asked, "Can you bring me a little luck, honeybunch?"

Flossy, knowing she could never win with an unpredictable player sitting beside her, excused herself from the table. Betty grabbed her arm and stage-whispered, "Don't go, Flossy, I need your luck, I need the cash…"

Embarrassed for her friend, whom she preferred sarcastic rather than pathetic, Flossy suggested, "Come on, sweetheart, let's go get some air, and then we can come back and play again."

"No way! No way I am leaving this lucky table. *You* go, and maybe the blackjack gods won't be able to tell the difference between you and me."

Fat chance, Flossy thought to herself. But aloud she said, "Go for it, honey, but remember, stand pat on fifteen, and you will leave less to luck." Heedless of this good advice, Betty waved her away.

Flossy joined Faith, Gladys, and Dottie at the roulette table, planning to waste a few dollars there just to be with her friends. She preferred blackjack, where remembering the cards and playing by the rules gave her more than a fifty-fifty chance of winning, whereas with roulette she might just as well have closed her eyes. So she closed her eyes and bet on number four, which was Norman's lucky number, and it hit for $100. The girls were ecstatic for Flossy, and she shared her bounty with them. They became partners for a while and soon lost it all.

They drifted around the casino. It was a long night for them, and they were ready to go home, but the boat sailed from seven until midnight, and there was no jumping in a taxi. "No jumping ship!" laughed Gladys. The champagne kept them going, but their collective heads were starting to ache. Most of them played the slot machines where they could sit comfortably and stare dumbly at the apples and oranges and not lose too much money. Flossy couldn't bear the slots, so she wandered back to the blackjack tables.

Only one of them had given up gambling altogether, as she truly could not afford it. She had pretended to enjoy the playing but did not, and she was under no illusion that she could make her big killing here. She smirked to herself at the expression. As she walked in from the deck, where she had been pondering her fate and clearing her head, she saw Betty approaching the cashier, her gait shambling and her face gray.

"Sweetie, you look awful. Do you want me to go to the ladies' room with you?"

"Of course not. I can go myself. What a good idea. I need to have a good pee and splash some water on my face, and I will be as good as new. Here—take my bag. I never know what to do with it in the john. Hold it for me, and I will be right out."

A gift! she thought, and she thought fast. She dashed over to the cashier, took out Betty's platinum American Express card, and asked for $5,000 in chips. She knew she would be asked for ID, but she was pretty sure that all old ladies with blonde hair looked alike to the cashier. She smiled sweetly and proffered Betty's license, and just as she thought, he barely looked at it. She asked for $500 chips because she could easily slip ten into her bag. In a half hour, she would come back and turn them back in for cash. Brilliant! Betty would never remember how much she spent tonight.

As she turned away from the cashier, Betty was right behind her and glaring.

"You jus' yooshed *my* card!" Luckily her speech was so slurred she was not loud, and no one paid attention.

"Honey, I did not. You are so cockeyed you can't tell if it's my card or yours, my bag or yours." She steered Betty out to the deck, cajoling and sweet-talking. She explained very precisely, as if to a child, that she bought some more chips for herself while she was waiting, and she had her own bag in her hand and Betty's over her shoulder, so she could not possibly have mixed them up. "But, I admit, our bags do look a lot alike. No wonder you got so upset," she soothed.

But Betty was not convinced. Betty tried to wrest her bag away from her, clawing at the inside pockets. As they struggled, Betty unearthed a $500 chip and, holding it aloft, screamed, "You... you...you would *never* buy five-hundred-dollar chips, *never*! I know you. You are much too careful." She started pushing her friend and accusing her, louder and louder, of stealing her card. But Betty could hardly stand up, and the ship had started to roll. Rain began to pelt down on them, and the wind blew up, roiling the water below. The deck became slippery in the few minutes that they tussled. There was no one in sight. With the next roll of the ship, it was not hard to tip Betty over the railing. And grab back her $500 chip...

She threw Betty's pocketbook in after her and headed straight to the ladies' room. Now *she* needed to splash some water on her face. "Calm, calm, calm," she told herself. She was not used to acting so spontaneously—either out of anger or fear—and yet she did, being both furious and petrified. She could not believe that crass Betty, of all people, might have ruined it all. "Stupid, stupid, stupid Betty—you did not have to die for this—and you never would have realized I 'borrowed' five thousand dollars. Why did you have to be so confrontational? Because you saw me, you did, so of course I couldn't allow that."

She sat on the toilet, fully dressed, breathing slowly in and out, in and out. "No one else saw you, no one else saw you, no one else saw you." She rocked back and forth repeating her mantra and slowly gathered her wits. It's not that she would miss Betty, but she was sorry she didn't plan better. No more spontaneous combustion. The next time, and she was quite sure there would be a next time, she would plan to the last detail—just as she did before. This time she would get away with it because she was lucky, not smart. No one, no one would be surprised that Betty had an accident; she was drunk as a skunk. Just then the boat pitched, and she almost slid off the toilet seat. "My luck holds!" she exclaimed to the weather gods. "You are making it storm, and everyone must have felt that lurch. How easy would it be for an unbalanced old lady leaning over the rail to lose her footing? And disappear."

CHAPTER THIRTY

She brushed her hair, freshened her face, and went out to find the girls, stopping first to cash in her chips. There was hardly anyone around, and she presumed everyone was getting in the last half hour at the tables before the boat docked. Just as she was stashing the last of her five crisp $1,000 bills into her Cucci-not-Gucci wallet, she bumped into Flossy.

"Hi there, Floss. Are you cashing in already too?"

"I am," said Flossy. "I am dog-tired, and I have won more than I deserve. I need to find a sofa to relax and put my feet up. Did you notice it's really hard to find a comfortable place to sit without gambling? I almost fell into the lap of Mitzi's cute croupier when the boat lurched, but that was not the comfort I was seeking." Flossy laughed regretfully. "So how did you do?"

"Not bad, not bad—I won a few hundred," she casually replied. "But you must have done well...*more than you deserve*?"

"Oh, I don't think I *deserve* any amount. But I am a careful gambler. I watch the cards, I never bet when I should fold, and I usually come out ahead, but this time I rocked!" With that, the boat rocked too, and they both laughed.

"I have just learned that expression from my great-granddaughters—you know, the ones who are twelve and ten. They have taught me, 'say whaaaat?' and 'wassup' as well, but I haven't found the appropriate venue for them...yet. I may get left behind in technology, but not in vocabulary!"

"So how much *did* you win?"

"Actually, I won $1,134, twice what Frances predicted!"

"Frances predicted you would win, um, $567?"

"She did, and I promised her if I won that amount I would give her half. Now I am going to give her the full amount and still get to keep $567 for myself." Flossy smiled, quite pleased with herself.

"So, Flossy, I guess you know what Frances is going to say when you give her the money: 'Say whaaat?'"

They both laughed and linked arms as they walked to the lounge area in search of a place to rest their weary bones and brains. "You really are so generous, Flossy. I admire you for that."

"Only to people I really care about, like Frances, and you, my friend."

"So what are you being generous about, Floss? Can I share?" asked Dottie.

"Uh-oh, I hear a spiel coming for your latest charity. 'Wassup?'"

The two women fell giggling onto a sofa, and Dottie didn't get the joke. "It's nothing, nothing—we are just overtired, and we are acting like children," Flossy proclaimed, disavowing their behavior.

Shortly, all the girls had gathered in the lounge, anxious to be the first ones off the gangplank so they could collapse at home and sleep. Already slightly hung over and exhausted, they couldn't wait to thank Betty for a won-der-ful night and crawl into bed. But so far Betty had not appeared.

None of them was worried, assuming Betty was getting in her last roll of the dice and last glass of champagne. Their only worry was the usual one, "How is she going to drive home?"

"Maybe one of us should drive her, and we can come back tomorrow for her car. Flossy, you can convince her to do it."

"I know, I know, and I will. I hate it when she gets so sloppy drunk. She loses all her dignity. It's not as if any of us is that dignified these days with our bodies failing and our brains deteriorating, but she has become piteous as a drunk. Has anyone noticed?"

They all nodded in agreement as Flossy told about Betty's behavior at the blackjack table.

This is just purr-fect, she thought to herself. *It's as if Flossy is my unwitting accomplice, she is setting this up so beautifully.*

But now it was fifteen minutes past midnight. The boat had docked, and most of the other people had departed, and still no Betty. A young mariner approached the girls and asked why they were not debarking. "We seem to have lost our friend," Mitzi confided coquettishly.

He responded at once, looking into her eyes. "We'll give the ship a thorough search. She probably just fell asleep somewhere and did not even notice we had stopped sailing. I mean, this happens to a lot of younger people too," he stammered, falling all over himself. "Why don't you ladies go on home, and we will send her home by taxi when we find her. I can see that you are exhausted." He had put his foot in his mouth again. "I mean not that you *look* it, it's just I did see you all yawning." He was making matters worse, but they appreciated his caring.

"Well, I don't think we can leave her like that," replied Flossy. "After all, it's *her* birthday party we are celebrating tonight. We will just settle down here and wait until you find her, right, girls?"

"If you say so, Floss." They were dying to leave, but they settled back down. They began to nod, and before long, Flossy, Faith, Dottie, Babs, Mitzi, and Gladys were all snoring lightly.

The young mariner tapped Mitzi on the shoulder, and she awakened with such a start they all popped open their eyes. His eyes regarded them tenderly, but they could tell he had bad news. "Oh my God," keened Gladys, "she must be dead!"

"No, no, ladies, we just can't find her. We have looked everywhere. The entire crew has been searching for over a half hour in every nook and cranny, in the bathrooms, and even under the gaming tables. She has disappeared. Are you sure she didn't leave without you?"

"We all planned to meet here in the lounge, but she was pretty…um…under the weather when we all last saw her. Do you think she could have gotten off the boat with the crowd before us and just driven herself home?" asked Faith.

They all ran to the railing and saw that Betty's car was still parked in the lot. "But she could've taken a cab," suggested the young man. "There are always a dozen or so that meet the boat when we dock."

At this point the captain entered the lounge, along with the ship's nurse. They had had traumas on board before, from heart attacks to insane reactions to big losses, but nothing quite like this. They tried to offer solace; they offered everything they could, from Valium to rides home, but the girls would not accept, nor would they accept that their friend had disappeared.

"Captain, can you lend me your cell phone?" asked Flossy, now alert and ready to take charge.

"Of course, madam."

First she tried Betty's home number, but only the machine picked up. Hoping against hope, she left a message to call her *whenever* she listened to her voice mail, no matter what time it was. Flossy then called Betty's building and asked the doorman if Betty had come in. The answer was a somber "no." Flossy handed the cell phone back to the captain and tried to be brave for her friends. "We *know* there must be a logical explanation for this," she pronounced. "So we will leave and let these nice people go home, and by tomorrow morning, this will all be straightened out. Right?" she asked, but she did not feel as confident as she sounded.

The girls trooped off the ship, slowly and quietly in the rain. They had been slow before, but rarely so quiet. They all felt the ominous gloom in the air and felt something terrible must have happened to Betty. No one would articulate it, but it was pretty obvious to all that in her drunken state, Betty must have fallen overboard.

When Flossy finally arrived home, she could barely stand up. As Frances helped her undress and tucked her into bed, Flossy told the story of the evening. Betty's disappearance was so upsetting that Frances could not bring herself to tell Flossy of her own terrible evening, although she had been waiting for hours to cry in Flossy's arms and be consoled. She swallowed her misery, and to take Flossy's mind off Betty, she asked, "So, *chica*, did you win?"

"Mmmmmm, yes, I had almost forgotten with all my worries about Betty. I'll pay you $567 in the morning."

"But you are only supposed to give me half," Frances prompted.

"I *am* only giving you half, my Francesca. Don't think because I'm tired that I don't remember my promises or my numbers. I won big—$1,134. You saw the future, but you only saw your half of the winnings. So in the morning we will share." Flossy hoisted herself up on one elbow and asked, "Can you see what happened to Betty?"

"No, no, my Flossita. I just had a lucky guess, but I will bet you that Betty will be fine in the morning…you will see. Now close your eyes and you will tell me all about how you won in the morning and I will tell you…"

But Flossy was already asleep.

CHAPTER THIRTY-ONE

"Why can't a woman be more like a man?"
— Henry Higgins

Roberto was driving so slowly he could have been mistaken for one of the senescent residents of South Ocean Boulevard. He had already met with almost all of the girls who had been with Betty the night before, and he was delaying his visit to the last, Flossy.

So far, having interviewed the boat crew and the girls, he had developed no leads, but he already had an inkling of what had happened to Betty. He was sure Flossy would have no new knowledge, but as a key potential witness, he knew he had to talk to her. Besides, she was a most observant woman..."*Ai*, and she probably realizes there is something wrong between Frances and me." He thumped his head with his hand and then pounded on the steering wheel as if to knock some sense into himself. "How did I let this happen?"

As he pulled into the driveway, he rehashed, for the twentieth time, what had happened between him and Frances. He had trusted her and confided his deepest unhappiness, and she had turned it against him...sort of. Because why? Did he not make it clear to her that she was different for him from any other woman he had known? Why did she not believe him? What was she afraid of? Why did she doubt him? *Why? Why? Why?* And at that moment when he was so vulnerable. And yet, and yet, maybe she was right? And is that why he got so angry? That he could not face the truth about himself? And maybe he wouldn't be able to fully commit to her? "*Dios mio*, this is the hardest mystery I have ever had to solve. Don't let me lose her."

"Excuse me, sir, who did you say you wanted to see?" asked the perplexed doorman, who had been carefully watching this man talking to himself as he approached the building.

Roberto flashed his badge and asked for Mrs. Kane.

"Yes, sir—503 North."

"I know, I know," said Roberto as he took a deep breath and marched staunchly into the elevator. He wished the elevator ride would give him more time to regroup, but alas, he arrived.

Flossy answered the bell, and with eyebrows arched, she rolled her eyes in the direction of Frances's room and pointed as she mouthed, "Go!"

"Who am I not to listen?" he humbly whispered, kissing her cheek.

And he found Frances leaning on the vanity in the bathroom, staring at herself in the mirror. Like Roberto, she had rehashed the previous night's debacle over and over again. In telling it all to Flossy as soon as she woke up, she was mortified by her own lack of control and was, more than ever, deeply miserable. How could she have let this chance go by? Would he ever forgive her? But… but what if she was right? What if he was so set in his ways he would never commit? So who cared? Why couldn't she just enjoy what she had for now? Why did she have to be such a—a *woman*? She was a big girl with almost grown children. Her career had exposed her to the best and often the worst of human behavior. Why couldn't she just accept the joy of the moment? Because… because she loved him, and with love came the fear of losing it.

She saw him over her shoulder in the mirror and melted.

"I am so sorry," they both cried out at once. And they threw themselves into each other's arms and kissed and cried and held one another, learning on the spot how to make up from their first fight.

"I can't believe I said what I did!"

"I can't believe I got so angry!"

"I would never want to hurt you."

"I would never want to hurt *you*."

"I think it's because...because we care so much," breathed Frances.

"I think it is because we never want to lose each other," murmured Roberto.

They held each other's faces, watching the tears rolling down their cheeks, and started to laugh. "*Ai*, Cisco!"

"*Ai*, Pancho, we both need some Visine!"

And sighing, they walked out to find Flossy, arm in arm.

"Well, you two," said Flossy, "it's good to see smiles on your faces. You two should get used to a little disagreement."

"*A little disagreement*!" they both shouted at once.

"It was hardly *little*..."

"You should've heard what she said..."

"Children, children, stop!" commanded Flossy, holding up her hand like a traffic cop. "It's rare I get to be the boss around here anymore with Frances monitoring my every move."

They laughed at her and held on to each other, knowing that their insecurities would not go away but that they had already taken steps in the right direction.

Holding hands, because they could not quite let go of each other, they settled down with Flossy to discuss the strange disappearance of Betty.

"What have you learned?" asked Flossy.

"Honestly, probably not much more than you knew last night, I'm afraid," replied Roberto. "I have interviewed the captain and crew, the croupiers, the wait staff, the cashiers. Those who even noticed her at all just confirmed what the rest of your friends have told me. Well, except for one embarrassing incident. She was *very* tipsy, as you know, and after you left her at the blackjack table, Flossita, she actually propositioned the croupier. He was so flustered he didn't know what to do, so he told his table he had to go on his break, and he ran to the men's room to hide from her. We know she skulked around for a while, because he kept peeking out. The poor fellow is only twenty-four years old, and this was way beyond his ability to cope. Can you imagine this kid hiding in the men's room from an eighty-four-year-old lady? She must have lost interest after about fifteen minutes, or forgotten what she was hanging around there for, because when he next looked out, the coast was clear, and he dashed back to his table.

"So, on my timeline, because this young croupier was looking at his watch to see how long he was stuck in the bathroom, this was about ten fifty. The next time we know anything of her whereabouts is from the cashier, who believes he saw her about eleven o'clock, when she bought five thousand dollars worth of chips. He told me he was surprised, because most old ladies—excuse me, Flossita, present company excluded—rarely buy that much, and even if they do, they don't ask for five-hundred-dollar chips but prefer smaller denominations so they can make it last longer. Then he said she came back around eleven thirty and cashed the chips back in. He thought it was strange in hindsight, but at the time he was getting ready to close up and thinking of going home, so he didn't say anything—like, 'How come you have the exact same amount as I sold you a half hour ago?' But he told me he sees all kinds of peculiar behavior, and it was quite likely she had a cup of coffee and changed her mind about spending the money. Who knows? It's foolish to speculate, and this is hardly a definitive clue."

"That's it?"

"Well, for now. We have the boys from our station, plus West Palm and Manalapan, canvassing the other guests on the boat with Betty's picture, but the idea that anyone saw anything is a long shot."

"So, *chico mio*, do you think she just *fell* overboard?"

"It's not hard to imagine, given her state of equilibrium. There was a fairly rough rainstorm that blew in a bit after eleven, as you know, Floss, and it caused the boat to rock pretty hard a few times, according to the captain. So she could have been leaning over the side, um, you know, spilling her cookies."

"Spilling her cookies? Does that mean vomiting in police procedural terms?" asked Flossy, looking quite serious.

"Um, yes, I just didn't want to say it, as it is such a disgusting, sad picture that it evokes, your spunky but drunk friend being sick all over herself, so I guess I cleaned it up a bit."

"No need to clean it up for me, Roberto, honey. I can handle it. And I know the boat was rocking for a bit. I had trouble keeping my balance *inside* the cabin. I think you are probably right. The boat just listed to one side and over she went. Or she could just have fallen down and slid right under the railing, you know? Trying to get a grip on the slippery metal, scrambling for purchase, panicking with no one to hear her in the wind and rain..."

"Oh, Flossy, I shouldn't have to worry about putting pictures in your mind. Your imagination is vivid enough."

"Do you think—I mean, you must have to consider this—do you think she could have been pushed?"

"Of course I have to consider it, but Flossy, what would be the motive? The poor young croupier may never flirt with an older woman again, but he surely was not embarrassed into murder. Who else? Why?"

"Ro-ber-to, you know Frances and I have had our suspicions right here among our friends."

"Flossy, stop right now. Now I am being the cop because I am the cop. Your friends are dying because they are old, and sometimes confused, and most recently because this one could not hold her liquor. Frances has told me that all of you were terrified that she would die in a car accident one of these nights, DWI. At least this way she did not take anyone with her."

"Do you think her body will show up?" asked Frances.

"Possible. With the storm, the tides are less predictable, and of course we don't know exactly when or where she fell, so actually, I hope not. Bodies that spend days, or even hours, in the sea are not pretty to look at. Better her family remember her the way she was."

At that moment, Roberto's cell phone rang, and he walked inside to take the call. Frances and Flossy held hands as if they were two chastised children.

"Her pocketbook has floated ashore in Boca."

"How do you know it was hers?"

"Because her wallet was in it with her license."

"Any money in it?"

"I know what you are thinking...no. Her wallet did not have five thousand dollars in it, but there was one section of the pocketbook wide open, so the cash could have been shoved in there and floated away. Lots of other female pocketbook contents were missing as well—you know compact, lipstick, cell phone. Only her wallet and car keys were in the closed portion."

"I don't know, I think she would have put the money in her wallet."

"Flossy—she was dead drunk!" insisted Roberto, not a little bit frustrated with his amateur detectives.

"Um, and now she is just dead dead," observed Flossy woefully.

CHAPTER THIRTY-TWO

"Morris and Izzie love baseball. Every day they sit on a bench by the boardwalk and argue about the Red Sox and the Yankees, but mostly they reminisce about their younger days when they played sandlot ball. And those days were long, long ago. They are widowers, most of their friends have died, and their children are always so busy. But at least they have each other; they have been friends since grade school."

"Hey," interrupted Max, "I thought this was supposed to be a joke. You're starting to make me cry."

"It is, it is, don't be so impatient," admonished Sy. "I'm just setting the scene.

"One day, Morris is feeling philosophical and asks, 'Izzie, I wonder if there is baseball in heaven? Because, Izzie, my buddy, my spiritual brother, you know one of us is going to die first. It's going to be really lonely for the one left alone. If you go first, will you try to communicate with me and tell me what it's like up there? Will you tell me if there is *baseball*? I will miss you so much.'"

"I can't take this," protested Max.

"Be quiet and listen!" chastised Sy, continuing with the story. "With his eyes tearing up, Izzie promises to communicate, and he exacts the same promise from Morris, should he go first.

"Alas, a few months later Izzie has a heart attack and dies. Morris is bereft. He goes to their favorite bench every day and replays last night's game as if Izzie were with him. One day he hears a voice. *Can it be Izzie?* No, of course not, it's just his imagination. He knows their promises were just sentimental slop. But he hears the voice again, and this time he is sure it sounds just like Izzie. 'Izzie, is it you…is it really you?'

"'It is, and I am in heaven, Morris. It is better than we could ever have imagined up here. I have seen all the old gang, my mother, and my father. I live in a beautiful place, the food is good…'

"Morris interrupts. He is beside himself with curiosity. 'But tell me, Izzie, is there *baseball* in heaven?'

"'Well, Morris, I have some good news and some bad news. The good news is that there *is* baseball in heaven. The bad news is…you're pitching on Thursday!'"

The men chortled at the preposterousness of the joke. They were pretty cynical about the idea of an afterlife, but they loved the vision of the best friends being reunited on the baseball diamond in heaven.

They were standing around the outside of the funeral home watching the girls walk slowly to their cars. Like their group, the girls' group had become smaller in the last few years, and most recently in the last few weeks. Bunny, Caroline, Paula, and now Betty were gone. How could anyone not ponder who would be next? Better to turn to more temporal subjects as they joined the girls.

"That was a lovely eulogy, don't you think, Sy," commented Dottie.

"Puh-leez, Dot," said Babs before Sy could answer. "*Who* were they talking about? Our Betty? They made her into a saint!"

"But Babs, dear," interjected Sy, "that's how her children want to remember her. Who cares, if that's what makes them happy? And it was a kind and loving eulogy," he added, defending Dottie.

"You are right, of course, Sy," said Flossy, "but I think what I objected to most was that they took all her personality away.

There was nothing of the feisty, funny, sardonic lady we knew and loved."

"Most of the time," added Faith.

"And furthermore," suggested Mitzi, "maybe she *used* to be the warm and loving woman they described—I mean when she was young, before we knew her."

"That would be surprising from what we know of her kind thoughts about her late husband," retorted Babs.

Gladys was surprisingly quiet, especially since she and Betty both came from the same hometown. Now they turned to her for a firsthand opinion, and she resisted. "I really don't want to talk ill of the dead…"

"But Gladie, you can tell *us*. You know we were her friends no matter what," cajoled Faith. "Really, honey, you don't *have* to say anything, but we would like to know. In fact, it might help us understand why she could be so mean to us out of the blue and maybe why she drank too much as well."

"All right, I guess it won't hurt anybody now. You see, Betty actually mellowed in her old age. Gossip had it that her mother had a nasty tongue, and so did the whole family. Their reputation went all the way back to the *shtetl* in Russia. I can see *my* mother shaking her finger at me now. 'Gladys, you be polite when you go over there. You wouldn't want to fall into that Mrs. Greenstein's mouth…'"

The girls nudged her on, before she got lost in the memory.

"Okay. So what happened, I think, is that poor Mel had no idea what he had let himself in for. Or maybe he thought he could tame her. Well, he couldn't, so what he did do was never come home. Lots of people were pretty sure there was a quiet, sweet thing on the side. I mean, who would blame him, having to come home to Betty haranguing him all the time. Sooooo, according to *my* children, she took out all her frustrations on her kids. Those two may have told the rabbi nice things about her, after all, she *was* their mother, but they were battered."

"*Really* battered?" asked Mitzi. "I feel terrible for them."

"What's really battered? It doesn't have to be physical. Can you imagine having a mother tearing you down all the time? It's amazing they're both successful adults," answered Gladys.

"Hmmmm...not surprising that one is an analyst and the other lives on the other side of the world, as far away as he could get, I guess," noted Flossy.

"Well, I'm going to go right over and give them big hugs right now," announced Mitzi. She marched off in a flourish of chiffon and enfolded Betty's boys in an ample embrace. The other girls followed suit, and the men walked behind. They offered the boys firm handshakes and pats on the back. They were all anxious to leave, as were Betty's children.

But one, Robert, the analyst, stopped Flossy and said, "You know my mother really enjoyed your friendship."

Taken aback, Flossy replied, "Thank you for telling me. It's a lovely thing to say, but how do you know?"

"My mother was not easy, as I am sure you know, but she did have a heart somewhere beneath that bravado, and she also was a discerning woman. She thought you truly cared about her, and I believe you did."

"Well, you are right, Robert. I did care for your mother. She could be hard, but she did not frighten me. Yes, she angered me sometimes, but mostly I was sad for her. I don't think she was very happy, although I think our gang of girls gave her pleasure. She was so excited to take us all on the gambling boat for her birthday."

"Was she so drunk, do you think, that she could actually have hurled herself overboard?"

"Robert, you are the analyst, and I believe you are careful with your words. The way you said that, am I to infer you think she purposely *jumped* overboard?"

"I don't know. I find it hard to believe she just slid off the deck. And her drinking, which, I've been told, got worse in the last year, could easily have been to mask her pain. Maybe she didn't know any other way to get rid of it; the drinking wasn't working, and so she just…"

"Maybe you have seen a different side of your mother than we have these last few years, Robert. Your mother, despite her cynical, sometimes even very hurtful comments, may not have been happy, but in a way she was optimistic. She always thought that the next day might bring a new opportunity. A new man, in fact. She didn't have much luck, but she was still hoping."

"Oh God, no. I never saw that, nor did I ever hear her say that she would be interested in a relationship with a man. In fact, I haven't seen much of my mother over these last few years to talk to her about anything. It's been easier for me not to deal with her disapproval of my celibacy while trying to raise my kids, of my career, of my kids' behavior, of just about everything I have ever done. I am sure you can imagine how unsupportive she could be. When my father wasn't around to bully, my brother and I were always next in line. You might surmise that when he died she would have let up on us, but she didn't. I guess it had gotten to be a habit by then. We never got the chance, or maybe as adults we never tried enough, to see her as a real human being, nor did she try to have a humane relationship with us as adults.

"I probably help patients in my situation much more than I have ever helped myself…but I guess one is always the child of a parent, no matter how old one gets, nor how mature we think we are. And I am regretful, hugely regretful."

"But Robert, you must have *some* good memories…you said to me that she had a heart."

"You know, the one time I can remember her being kind to me was during my divorce. In hindsight, it may have been because she admired my making the break. Interestingly, despite the vitriol she handed out to me when I chose my wife, she never said 'I told you so' when I decided to end my marriage. She just comforted me and encouraged me to move on. Looking back, I guess she was helping me do what she could not do herself. Oh, I feel awful about staying away from her. I feel awful about her wanting and hoping to have some romance in her life. And I don't blame her for not finding it with my father." Smiling wryly, Robert wiped his eyes, and Flossy held him for a few moments.

"Robert, you have a long, good life ahead of you and two beautiful children. Don't waste it with regrets. Find a woman to love and who will love you, and your mother will be happy wherever she is."

"Knowing my mother, she will bully herself out of heaven to let me know what she thinks of the next woman I choose!"

"I have no doubt you are right, Robert, but in the meantime, I'll give you a call in a week or so to see how you are doing."

"Thank you, Flossy, my mother cared for you for good reason."

"So, Flossy, you are expanding your family yet again," commented Faith as she linked arms with her.

"I can't help it. I like staying in touch with my friends' children. Do you know that Zoë told me the other day that she ran into the daughter of an old friend of mine who repeated verbatim the conversation she'd had with me over fifteen years ago. I was calling her after her mother, Ida, died and just making small talk. I asked if she was seeing anyone or if she wanted to be fixed up with anyone..."

"Oh no, Flossy, were you trying to make a match with your nephew Lionel back then?"

Smiling sheepishly, Flossy admitted, "I was, but what happened was that this young woman told me she was *gay*. Well, to say the least I was taken aback, as she had already been married and had two children. I gulped and said, 'Well, Lizzie, I'll try to find you a cute woman.'"

They laughed at Flossy's solution and walked off together to find the rest of the gang.

CHAPTER THIRTY-THREE

You see a lot of smart guys with dumb women, but you hardly ever see a smart woman with a dumb guy.

— Erica Jong

The girls piled into Mitzi's Jaguar. With Dottie going off with Sy to a matinee, the rest—Flossy, Faith, Babs, and Gladys—could squeeze into one car. They saw Sam Rabin hustling toward them, and Mitzi gunned the motor and peeled out of the parking lot.

"Whew! That was quite an escape," declared Babs, who, sitting in the middle, was thrown into Flossy's lap. "I feel like I am in the movies. What was that all about?"

"*Oy*!" moaned Mitzi. "That guy will be the death of me. I mean I hope not, but you know what I mean. He seems to be coming back after me. I thought I had dropped him, and he did disappear for a while. I figured he found someone else, but now he is *back*. He leaves six messages a day on my voice mail."

"Oh come on, Mitzi, you know you like the attention."

"I do *not*. You do not know what this man is like. He's impossible. He talks endlessly about nothing. He doesn't *read*. He is not interested in politics, in theater, in bridge..."

"How bad can he be? He's rich, he has his hair, he drives at night, he's healthy, he's..."

"Let me tell you," sniggered Mitzi, "if I had ten minutes left on earth, I would want to spend it with Sam Rabin."

"Wait a minute, you *would* want to spend it with Sam Rabin?"

"Yes, because *ten minutes with Sam Rabin seems like a lifetime*!"

The girls burst into laughter. They had just been to a funeral, but they did not feel disrespectful. They knew that laughter was the best antidote for their sadness and anxiety.

Recovering, Gladys recalled, "You know, I learned you can laugh after a funeral long, long ago at my grandmother's shiva. I was just sixteen years old, and it was my first funeral. I was so nervous. I didn't know how people would behave or how I should behave. What if everyone was sobbing? How would I comfort my father, whom I had never seen crying? I was *petrified*."

"No, sweetie, the *body* was petrified; you were just scared," observed Babs. "So what happened?"

"Oh, Babs, don't be so exact, I *felt* petrified. Although the coffin was open, my mother would not let me look at the body, and if she had, I probably would have fainted right then and there. But it was okay—everyone cried very discreetly, and I got a sense that this would be a dignified occasion. I tried to act very mature and solemn.

"When we got home for the shiva, people started pouring into the house. There was lots of talk—no one sat around acting like the end of the world. Suddenly my father said to the group around him, 'Did I ever tell you about Uncle Harold's funeral? I was young and nervous, and Aunt Henrietta dragged me over to the coffin. There he lay, my first *dead* body. I expected him to look all shriveled and gray, but he just looked like he was sleeping. *So,* prodded Aunt Henrietta, *so how does he look?*

"'Relieved that I had been able to look at a dead body and not pass out, I said, *He looks great, knock wood!* And I tapped my knuckles against the nearest piece of wood—the coffin!'

"My father and the crowd roared at the artlessness of his youth. I loved the story of my father being so young and awkward, and I always thought he told the story for me.

"Many years later when my father died, the family all met at the funeral home to make plans. The funeral director took us into a huge room filled with coffins on display. We had to choose one for my father. Would he have liked blue or white satin? Mahogany or oak? Brass fittings or copper? If we did not like any of the floor models, we could have one custom designed. It was like…like buying a new car, but my father, my father was dead. Sadly you all know what it was like—being in that stifling and airless room with those deep-maroon velvet curtains covering the windows, gloomy lighting, Kleenex boxes placed so tactfully on all the side tables. You feel like you have to speak in whispers as the funeral director does his lugubrious best to sell you a coffin that will last forever—you know, with his hands clasped religiously in front of him. Anyway, as we drifted among the coffins trying to decide how to choose, I noticed that aside from the door we had entered, there was only one other door. It was posted with a forbidding sign, NO EXIT. As my brother and I caught each other's eye, we had the same thought at the same moment—Dad would have loved this! No exit from the coffin room. We burst out laughing, and we could not stop. The more the funeral director, with his faux sympathy, looked at us, the more we laughed. My mother started glaring, and when we pointed to the sign, she too fell into a fit of giggles, and so on with my husband and sister-in-law. It really was not *that* funny, but the weirdness of the situation, the fact that our emotions were so close to the surface, the fact that the funeral director was clearly thinking he had a bunch of crazies on his hands, just made us laugh more.

"Why is it that funeral homes have to be so somber and funeral directors have to be so dour? When you bury me, I don't want a service at a funeral home. I am *serious*. Just have me cremated and scatter me around the beach and into the sea."

"But Gladie, honey, if you are serious about this, what about your children?"

"They already know I detest funeral homes…I'll write them a letter tonight. But in case something happens today, you heard it from me here and now!"

"Gladie, nothing's going to happen today. You *should* write a letter, though."

"Hey, honeybunch, what if you meet someone, and he wants to carry your ashes around in his little Mercedes convertible?"

"Okay," conceded Gladys, "but he can't have all of me. Deal?"

"Deal," they all agreed.

"So, girls, what about the rest of you, what do you want?"

"Well, for sure I don't want my children spending my money for a fancy coffin," said Babs. "I have not been counting my pennies so they can spend it on ebony and silver that will molder in the ground for eternity. I guess I better write a letter too."

"But Babs, dear, do you want one of those plain pine coffins?"

"Uh, no, I guess not, but maybe I will go online to choose something reasonable."

"Hah…the *end* in online shopping! Pun intended," giggled Faith. "But do you really think you can find *coffins* online?"

"Honey, you can find *everything* online, and I mean everything. I bet I could find a good used one on eBay," replied Babs.

Mitzi chimed in, "I would like to be buried with a view, preferably something romantic."

"And have you specified that you should be wearing pink chiffon and Chanel number five?"

"In fact, I have. My children know they are to bury me looking great. You never know who you will meet…"

"Oh, silly Mitzi, you know our bodies will not meet anything; it's just over. So I don't care where or how, after I am dead. I want to focus my thoughts right here on earth," added Faith, with her usual common-sense point of view.

"Well, my intellect knows that Faith is right, but my soul, presuming I have one, holds out a small hope of some spiritual continuance," considered Floss. "And just in case, I want you to bury me with two decks of cards!"

"Now that's an idea...bridge to heaven, or something like that," approved Mitzi. "So what do you think Dottie would say if she were here?"

"I wouldn't be surprised if she had already worked out her own eulogy about how she cared about all the downtrodden of the earth, the bringing together of Christians and Jews, peace on earth, recycling, Democrats, etc., etc. She probably will have her kids pass out contribution envelopes," answered Babs. "You know, *In lieu of flowers the family of Dorothy Dornbush suggests you make a contribution to save the world like she did.*"

"Babs, are you taking on the mantle of Betty?" asked Mitzi.

"No, no, I'm sorry. I guess funerals just make me cranky. I don't really begrudge Dot's charitable ways. Maybe I just wish I had the wherewithal..."

"Hey, Babs, honey, you probably do have enough for that ebony coffin and charity balls, you just *choose* to be frugal," suggested Faith, trying to be nice.

But her comment was misinterpreted, and Babs took umbrage. "*You* do not know what I can and cannot afford!"

"Gee, Babs, I am sorry, really sorry. I only meant, I mean, I meant that you are careful, I mean thoughtful...I mean I should not have said that, and I am sorry. I just think a lot about how lucky we all are to afford this luxurious life. Am I forgiven?" asked Faith.

"Sure," said Babs as they blew air kisses at each other, but she did not quite sound so sure.

Flossy thought of intervening but realized that Babs would get over it and that all their nerves were a bit frayed at this point. So she veered the conversation away from money to love.

"Gosh, I wonder if, you know, because Dottie and Sy have been together for so long, if they plan to be buried next to each other or in their family plots."

"This is definitely an interesting situation," worried Mitzi. "Which husband should *I* be buried with?"

"Please, Mitzi. Your second husband's children wouldn't have you, the third you were glad to get rid of, so obviously you should be buried with the first who was the father of your children," said Flossy, quickly resolving the conundrum.

"Right you are for me. But what about Dot? Do you think she and Sy are discussing this at their matinee?" asked Mitzi salaciously.

"They were going to a *movie*," declared Faith.

"How do you *know* that? Don't you think matinees work better for old lovers? I mean, not that I would know, unfortunately," said Gladys.

"Oh honey, there is still time."

CHAPTER THIRTY-FOUR

"A Jewish couple is sitting together on an airplane flying to the Far East. Suddenly, over the public address system, the captain announces, 'Ladies and gentlemen, I am afraid I have some very bad news. Our engines have ceased functioning and this plane will be going down. Luckily I see an uncharted island below us that should be able to accommodate our landing. However, the odds are that we will never be rescued, and we will have to live on the island for the rest of our lives.'

"A few minutes later the plane lands safely on the island. Benny turns to his wife and asks, 'Esther, did we pay our capital campaign pledge to the Yeshiva yet?'

"'No, Benny,' she responds.

"Benny smiles and then asks, 'Esther, did we pay our United Jewish Appeal pledge?'

"'*Oy*, no! I haven't sent the check,' she says.

"Now Benny laughs out loud.

"'One last thing, Esther. Did you remember to send our Temple Building Fund check this month?' he asks.

"'*Oy*, Benny, I didn't send that one, either,' says Esther.

"Now Benny is practically choking with laughter.

"Esther asks Benny, 'So? Why are you so happy?'

"Benny answers confidently, 'They'll find us.'

"So my friends," said Mitzi, after she has told them the story of Benny and Esther, "are we serious about taking a cruise together this spring?"

Gathering up the cards from the table, where she had just won at bridge again, Flossy looked around at her friends and said, "I'm in! But it's going to take more than ten times my annual winnings to pay for it! And I think I have to take Frances."

"Flossy, don't you think you can manage without her for ten days?"

"I know I *can*—it's do I want to? I feel so secure when she is with me. She checks my heart and my respiration and of course administers my oxygen. She helps me bathe when I am exhausted and feeling weak, and she makes me get out of bed in the morning and eat breakfast. What am I thinking? Of course I will take Frances—life is too short for us these days to save money."

"Speaking of life being short," wondered Gladys, "I mean, we know we are not young; what if something happens to one of us on the cruise? Like a heart attack or something?"

Flossy tried to dispel Gladys's anxiety. "Oh, sweetie, they have the nicest, *best* doctors on these boats. I know because Norman got pneumonia on our last cruise. He could not go ashore for any of the excursions, and frankly he didn't care. He was not much of a sightseer anyway, and he and the ship's doctor—a very suave and sophisticated Englishman as I remember—spent the afternoons together swapping stories and, would you believe, playing pinochle!"

"Hmmmm, where do you think the suave English doctor's wife was?"

"Oh," replied Flossy, for a moment not catching Gladys's drift, "poor guy, he was a recent widower."

"I'm in!" cried Gladys and Mitzi simultaneously.

"Honey, he's *mine*," shouted Gladys. "You've had your beaux. I *need* him more." She began to fake cough, "See, I already need an appointment."

They all laughed and started to get excited about the trip. Faith brought out the various cruise brochures she had accumulated for them. "They all look wonderful, but do you think, I mean because we are a bunch of widows, that, you know, we won't fit in?"

"Don't be silly, Faithie, dear. If we can pay, we can fit in," replied Babs. "In fact, I *know* that some of these cruises are so filled with eligible widows like us that the crew includes some hosts."

"Hosts?"

"Yes, they are men of a suitable age who ostensibly are there as tour guides and lecturers, *but* they also have to be attractive and be willing and able to *dance*. So when we go to dinner and the band starts playing, we don't have to sit around like a bunch of wallflowers because all the *couples* are dancing, and we have no partners."

"You are kidding. You're making this up!" declared Faith, definitively.

"No, I am not…because I actually met one."

"Aha! Babs has a secret lover!"

"I do not," denied Babs, actually blushing. "Although of course I wish I did. I may not be out there like Gladys and Mitzi, but I wouldn't mind a spin around a dance floor from time to time, literally *and* metaphorically.

"I met him at a bookstore. I had my nose in a book about the Dalmatian coast, and he was browsing in the same area. He asked me which guidebook I thought was the best, and I asked him when he was going—you know, just making conversation. I found out he worked for one of the cruise lines, and I told him I thought it had to be the greatest job…I wished I could do that, but what job, after all, would a woman of my age be able to do? I admitted I was just browsing because of wanderlust, not because I was really going anywhere."

"So then he told you what his job was..." prompted Flossy.

"No, not exactly then," balked Babs, blushing again.

"Hey, did our Babs have a *date*?"

"Not really. We just went out for a cup of coffee together. He travels around the world three times a year and then fills in with short cruises...you know, down to South America or around the Mediterranean. He is only home two weeks a year."

"Cheez, what a life! Would you really want that?"

"No, not really. I would miss all of you, and I would miss seeing my children, but it works for him. He's a retired history teacher. He taught at Andover. He and his wife were both teachers there, in fact. They had one daughter who died in her twenties, tragically, in a car accident, and when his wife died he had no one, nothing. He told me he had no interest in life at all, until a friend told him about this job opportunity. He figured he had nothing to lose, and he's been seeing the world ever since. He could never have afforded to travel like he does on his teacher's retirement benefits, and he is such a kind, interesting man, with such a thirst for knowledge and a passion for communicating it that I bet he's terrific at his job. He told me he has some tedious, tedious nights with daffy or dull women, but often he meets interesting, nice people...like me."

"So did you ever see him again?"

"He does call me when he comes to town twice a year, and we go out for a bite, and he tells me about his adventures. We are just friends, really. I don't even know if he is a good dancer or not!" She smiled. "But I do look forward to his visits, and I do have a collection of cards from around the world that he has sent me."

"Babs, how long has this been going on?"

"Aha, my secret life, which is composed of five dinners and one coffee. So that's three years if you can count. And now you know all."

"No, we do not. Is he handsome?"

"Well, to me he is. If you must see for yourself, you will find him in one of Faith's brochures. Here, this one from Cunard."

They all gathered round, leafing through the pages of the brochure, until they came to a photo of an elegant couple standing on the deck in evening clothes. Babs smiled again.

"Babs, you little vixen, he is *gorgeous*!" proclaimed Mitzi.

And in truth he was classically handsome with silver hair and deep-blue eyes. Very well preserved indeed. "My God, he looks like a *model*, Babs!"

"Who would have thought that our straight and narrow accountant, Babs, would have a secret life with a handsome intellectual?"

Babs put on a pout and pretended to be insulted, but in fact she enjoyed sharing this particular secret with her girlfriends.

"So, Babs, dear, are you going to lobby for the cruise that *he* is on?"

"Honestly, I don't even know his schedule, and even more honestly, can you imagine pursuing my romance with my five chaperones?"

"But if you *really* don't know his schedule, we just might all get lucky and get to share him with you."

"Aaghh, no way I am sharing Jack with the lot of you unless I get to charge a finder's fee!"

"Hah…way to go, Babs, always figuring how to make a little money on the side. What is his name, anyway—Jack what?"

"He is John Charles Miner the *third*."

"*Oy*, so I guess he's not an Indian?"

"Is Babs going out with an Indian?" interrupted Frances, who had just come into the room.

"Oh, Frances, sweetie," explained Flossy, "Indian is our *code* word for Jewish—you know, a member of one of the twelve tribes in the Bible…hence Indian. It's what we say when we are in a public place and don't want to say, 'Do you think so-and-so is Jewish?'"

"Ohhhhh, I get it," said Frances. "So my little *meshuganah*, can I be an honorary Indian?"

Rolling her eyes at Frances's Yiddish, Flossy embraced her and responded, "Only if I can be an honorary Puerto Rican, Francesca. But before I kick you all out of here so I can pay my bills and take a nap, I'll tell you a funny story about misunderstanding racial labels. Years ago when our grandson was at Bowdoin College, Norman and I were out to dinner with him, and he told us that he had a girlfriend.

"'I am presuming she is not an Indian,' said Norman, who doubted there were any Jews besides his grandson at Bowdoin.

"'No, in fact she *is* an Indian,' our grandson replied.

"'No kidding,' said Norman, 'I can't believe you found the one Jewish girl on campus.'

"'I didn't. She is an Indian from *India*,' our grandson answered, a bit anxious about how we would react.

"I could see Norman gulp, but he recovered brilliantly and said, 'Well, any kind of Indian is fine with me, as long as you like her.' And everyone relaxed. We met her a year later at graduation and she was a lovely, beautiful girl."

"Did he mean it?" asked Dottie. "I mean about it being okay?"

"Of course he did. He later told me he had a vision of hundreds of years of Kane bar mitzvahs ending with his grandson's Hindu marriage ceremony, but it was just a momentary pang. We never cared about that—marrying Jews, or whites, for that matter. Truly, I think I am different from most of you in that way."

Frances nodded in agreement, knowing for sure that Flossy was different from her friends in that way. She was remembering how the girls had been so anxious to put the blame on *her* when Paula died.

"So he didn't marry her, did he?"

"No, he married a nice Irish Catholic girl!" laughed Flossy, smiling contentedly. "And I adore her. But hey, before you all go, we haven't decided anything. I say we make the final decision at dinner at the club on Friday night. Agreed?"

They all assented with thumbs up, except one.

"I don't know if I want to do this," said Dottie, who has been pretty quiet all afternoon. "I mean, it's not leaving Sy. He visits his kids every spring and then goes on a golf tour with the guys, but I mean, all these exotic ports, with terrorism and everything. What if we get kidnapped or taken hostage or something?"

"Honey, remember Benny and Esther. Just don't pay up any of your pledges—just think of all the charitable organizations that will come and find you!"

"Okay, I'm in too. I will just have to pledge double this year to make sure they send out a search party!" promised Dottie, her fear of her farfetched scenario evidently allayed by the excitement. "Let's choose on Friday so we can all make our down payments and get the staterooms we want, because if we don't book soon, gee, one of us could die!" Dottie pronounced in mock horror.

"*That is not funny*," they chorused, larking as they walked to the door.

CHAPTER THIRTY-FIVE

She lingered at Flossy's after the others had left, just chatting idly, reluctant to leave.

She knew she could never afford the cruise but desperately wanted to go. She was so daunted she thought she might ask Flossy's advice. Should she back out, using the excuse of a family wedding or needing dental implants or how about even a slight heart murmur? The girls would believe any of it. But maybe she could take out a loan? She could put up her apartment as collateral. Would the bank let her do it for something as frivolous as a cruise? God, she was miserable…

Why couldn't she just be content with what she had: a good, healthy life, not wanting for much. For God's sake, she was living and would likely die in Palm Beach, Florida, one of the most glamorous cities in America…in the world, even. But she was not content. "I am a greedy, greedy person," she said out loud.

"Huh?" said Flossy, who was sitting with her back to her as she paid bills at her desk. Flossy could not see what she said, so did not hear her.

"Nothing, nothing, Flossy," she yelled at her back. "I am just thinking out loud." She sat on the bed nattering to Flossy, wondering how to ask for help, wondering if she should honestly admit her uncomfortable position. Well, she could not be totally honest and admit everything, of course. She had killed, *killed* three people for much less money than she needed for the cruise. But those opportunities had just *presented* themselves. She could not have allowed Bunny's new bookkeeper to discover that she was using Bunny's credit card. It would just have been a matter of time—a short time—until the bookkeeper would be asking Bunny for receipts. And then of course, Flossy and Frances had coincidentally seen her at Saks making that first purchase with Bunny's card. That had been a close call, but it sure felt delicious to have the lovely things she wanted.

Then there was poor dear Paula. Killing her and using her credit card was just so easy. She could not resist taking advantage, and by then she already had a taste for the thrill. But there was that coincidental meeting, *again,* with Flossy and Frances, when they ran into her at the mall just as she had finished her luxury binge. And then last month, she hadn't even *planned* to kill spiteful, pathetic Betty. In fact, she had *tried* to go straight and dated that most boring of bores, Sam Rabin. She did get some nice jewelry out of that, but it was certainly not worth the tedium of having to be with him. Killing was far more exciting, and hell could not be worse than living the rest of her days with Sam Rabin. And then Betty's money had been a treat to spend—all cash, so no paper trail. She still had about $1,500 left, and she could scrape together $500 more for a deposit while she figured out where to get the rest. Hmmmmm…that could be a plan, temporarily anyway. No need to bare her poverty to Flossy.

"Sweetheart, did you want to talk to me about something? I am afraid I am being rude sitting here paying bills when I feel you want to talk."

"No, no, go ahead. I just have to run errands and then go home. Sometimes it seems like the late afternoon and evening go on and on. I guess I am reluctant right now to be off on my own. I'm sorry, Floss, for imposing."

"Don't be silly. I like your company too."

And Flossy meant what she said and at that moment hated herself for suspecting her dearest friend, so she proposed, "Hey, next Thursday, I promised Frances that she could go out with Roberto. There's a big police dinner or something; she is all excited. You know I don't usually go out when we have a game all afternoon, I am just too tired, so do you want to come over and keep me company?"

"I would love to, and I will bring dinner. I know how much you love to cook."

"Don't be silly. Frances will make us something."

"Nothing doing. Let her go to the hairdresser and get her nails done. We can help her get made up and dressed so she does the detective proud and see her off. Dinner is on me, including my specialty, yum-yum carrot cake."

"Honey, I don't know how to tell you this. I have to be honest after all these years of smiling at your cake...I hate carrots."

"No offense. You are so cute to have been so secretive all this time. You don't have to keep secrets from *me*. But you do really love chocolate, right?"

"Now you're on. Tuna fish sandwiches and chocolate cake. I am already looking forward to next Thursday. So are you excited about the cruise?" Flossy asked, having settled their plans and, she hoped, made her friend feel more welcome.

"I am, but I've never done this before. Say we decide to take the Mediterranean Cunard cruise. I saw the price list for staterooms and suites, but what do you think it will cost all-in?"

"Well, when Norman and I did this, we always took a suite on an upper deck, but as singles we don't need that. I would say—I have a brochure right here—that we would each be very comfortable in a simple veranda stateroom. It's nine thousand dollars, but that always gets discounted. So, say eight thousand plus single supplement is back up to ten thousand. Then add a hundred dollars a day for extra food and tips and another hundred a day for shopping and incidentals and we get to twelve thousand. Then for airfare, I doubt we can use miles in May to get to Europe, so figure another three to four thousand dollars for a grand total of fifteen to sixteen thousand dollars. Not bad for ten ultra-luxurious days in Europe. Lucky for us we don't have to do it on the cheap."

"But wait, Flossy, can you get business-class airfare for even *five* thousand dollars these days?"

"Not if you don't ask. First of all, most of the airlines have a *special* business-class airfare if you book ninety days in advance, so we have time. Alternatively, you can get a 'two-fer' with a lot of the airlines if you have an Amex platinum card."

"How do you know all this, Flossy?" And what she really was thinking was, *You are so facile with all this, you don't know how it stabs me in the heart. I don't know any of this, because during the long course of my marriage we traveled to Europe only twice, and when we did we rode in the back of the plane and found our way around Paris by metro and ate in cafés. It was what we could afford, because we saved and saved to retire in Palm Beach. So now that I am here, it makes me jealous instead of grateful...what a horrid woman I am.* But she smiled.

"Oh, sweetie, I count on *you* for so many things, like the best English novels. What are they called? You've read them all."

"The Booker Prize winners."

"See, travel, after bridge and golf, is my third favorite hobby. And I am so excited about being able to travel again, I am jumping out of my skin...and I get to go with my best friends! Of course I wish Norman were alive, but he's not, and I have to live with what *is*, not what I would wish.

"And last year, I almost died, but I didn't, and now I have Frances who keeps me healthy and alive for I don't know how much longer. So where I am, at this stage of my game, I couldn't ask for more, really." She jumped up as she used to when balance wasn't something she had to think about and almost fell over, but catching herself on the side of the desk, she pulled herself up and, smiling ruefully, curled up next to her friend on the bed.

"Now, if you stay a few more minutes, I will call American Express and find out how much a 'two-fer' will cost to—where does that boat leave from?"

"Venice, but we haven't *definitely* decided on this one."

"I know, I know, but we will all be at dinner on Friday, and I want to have the information at hand." With that Flossy dialed the number on the back of her Amex card and waited. She was holding it in her hand, and as they were now sitting beside each other on the bed, it was not hard to memorize the number. In fact, it started with 3713 just like hers did, and the expiration date was the same as hers. All she had to remember were the next eleven numbers and the security code, and it was not hard to do. The card was sitting right there in front of her while Flossy stayed on hold. She said the numbers to herself over and over until she knew them like a bridge hand.

When the agent came on the phone and Flossy began to talk, she excused herself and went to the bathroom, palming a pen from the desk. She hastily scribbled the numbers on her underwear, flushed the toilet, and returned, putting the pen back while Flossy was distracted on the phone.

"Just as I thought," exclaimed Flossy, pleased with herself. "We can fly from New York, round-trip on a two-for-one ticket for $7,946.46! I made a reservation for you and me. You can pay me when I get my bill, and I can cancel at any time if we choose a different cruise."

"For me? You darling girl. But what about Frances?"

"Oh, I know she will want to reserve for herself so she gets the miles to travel back and forth to Puerto Rico. I will make sure she gets the discounted business-class rate, because I won't let her fly in the back with all of us up front, and I will reimburse her, of course. You don't have a platinum card, do you?"

"No, I don't because I never thought the extra fee was worth it. You know me, watching my budget."

"Hah! Old ladies who are not lucky enough to live Palm Beach have to count their pennies. You just do it out of a sense of responsibility," Flossy chastened her friend affectionately. "You should think of getting one. You can often use it for upgrades for hotel rooms and lots of other perks, like these two-fers. It's worth the money."

Huh…like I ever go to hotels where I could use it, is what she thought, but instead she said, "You're right, Flossy. I'll get a platinum card too—and make up for lost time."

"Yes! I'm looking forward to Friday night when we engrave this decision in stone, so I can call my travel agent Saturday morning and reserve my stateroom!"

"You use a travel agent? You don't call direct?"

"I do. I know mostly everyone else does it direct or even online now, but she is an old friend of the family. I feel bad cutting her out, and it is one less hassle for me. And it doesn't cost me any more, because her fee comes from Cunard."

Hmmmm, she thought. *This gets better and better. They will never catch—or at least not right away—two reservations made with the same card. I already have a plan.*

CHAPTER THIRTY-SIX

From birth to age eighteen a girl needs good parents. From eighteen to thirty-five she needs good looks. From thirty-five to fifty-five she needs a good personality. From fifty-five on, she needs good cash.

— Sophie Tucker

On Friday night the girls had decided on the Cunard cruise in the Mediterranean. They had all gone about making their reservations, groaning over the cost but delighting at the prospect of ten days in Europe in the lap of luxury.

Now Thursday had arrived, and they gathered together at their bridge game.

"I'm already getting ready!" announced Mitzi as she wafted in with her arms filled with shopping bags from Neiman's, Saks, and Chanel.

"Honey, we are not going for almost four months—and Lord have mercy, what do *you* need?" asked Babs.

"First, everything is on sale. Second, I can't wear these old things. Third, I deserve it. Fourth, I need it. Fifth, it makes me happy to think about wearing these new clothes aboard a beautiful yacht, where—you know—I just might meet my next new husband!"

"And you were the one on Friday complaining about the cost!"

"I got over it."

"No kidding." They all laughed, not so much at Mitzi as with her.

"I hate to put a damper on your fantasy, Mitzi, but it is *not* a yacht. It's a small cruise ship. You will have to wait for Mr. Gotrocks to sail the Mediterranean on a yacht."

"Oh, Babs, you are doing accuracy patrol as usual; yacht, not-a-yacht, you know what I mean, and how I feel—*very* glamorous."

Proceeding to show off her purchases, Mitzi pretended to model one pastel outfit after another and swirled around the room. Each ensemble seemed to have a perfectly matching chiffon scarf.

"Gee, I wish I could shop like that," grouched Gladys. "I just can't seem to make everything go together like you do. And besides, I am beginning to think a woman needs a man like a fish needs a bicycle."

"Huh? Where did you get that from?"

"Gloria Steinem," Gladys asserted.

"Of course, easy for her to say. She always has one!"

"Come on, Gladys, I will take you shopping tomorrow," promised Mitzi. "I just can't buy any more for myself right now, so it will be almost as much fun helping you go wild!"

"C'mon, Mitzi, you could buy more if you wanted to," commented Faith.

"I know, I know, but somehow I feel guilty."

"Hah! You know what Erica Jong said about that? 'Show me a woman who does not feel guilty, and I will show you a man,'" Faith quipped.

"Okay, okay, you're right, but don't we all feel a wee bit guilty for spending frivolously?"

"This is not only a female thing," added Flossy. "For God's sake, girls, are we not Jewish? How many jokes can there be about Jewish guilt?"

"And on top of that," reminisced Dottie, "Sy and I met Sydney Pollack at a benefit a few years ago. What a doll he was, so accomplished and unpretentious. He was actually quite attentive…"

"What does this have to do with guilt, Dottie, dear? Were you guilty that you were flirting, and Sy had taken you there?"

"No, no, no. I was just thinking how adorable he was, and now he is dead, but to make my point, he told me the main reason he loved living in Los Angeles instead of New York was because there is no guilt there. He said in LA the wealth is all right *out there*, up front, where everyone can see it, whereas in the East people felt guilty about showing off, so everyone keeps it out of sight behind the façades of their Park Avenue apartments. He liked the honesty of the Los Angeles glitz—kind of disarming coming from such a modest man."

"Well then, he would approve of what we are doing," concluded Flossy. "Just think of it this way, it is SKI money."

Babs questioned, "Ski money? C'mon, Floss, none of us has gone skiing in forty years. What are you talking about?"

"Babsy, you are too literal." Flossy grinned.

But all the girls were looking at her, awaiting the punch line of the joke they did not get.

Keeping them on tenterhooks, Flossy hesitated, and then let them in on her new expression. "It stands for *Spend the Kids' Inheritance!*"

They were all glad to be in the new SKI club.

She had joined in the fun with the girls, but to keep her nervousness from showing, she had made herself busy, putting out snacks and clearing dishes. Since the bridge game was at her apartment, she hoped it seemed natural. As her anxiety mounted, she reviewed the scenario she had worked out. Flossy, with her kindhearted soul, would not make it through the night. She could not believe how easy Flossy had made it for her to go on this vacation of her dreams. Well, it was not the South Pacific, but pretty dreamy nonetheless. First, Flossy practically dropped the Amex card in her lap. How clever she had been to jot the numbers down on her nylon panties. But she probably would not have forgotten anyway, she was so galvanized by the opportunity. And she'd had to wash the underwear twice already to get out the black ink. It still showed a bit, but no one was watching her undress these days, so if a little ink still showed, who cared?

Then, so trusting and so generous, Flossy had bought her plane ticket. That was the catalyst for her plan. She would reserve her place on the boat online pretending to be Flossy, but make the reservation in her own name, just like making plane reservations for her kids to come down and visit or sending a gift online. She already knew Flossy's maiden name and the high school she attended from all the stories Flossy told about her youth. She even knew her mother's maiden name—Horowitz. She knew these were the typical security questions asked. But the reservation went through, no questions asked. She even got Flossy a ten percent discount for booking early. The irony of it. And how about the coincidence of Flossy inviting her over for the evening? No poisoning the cake this time—Flossy was much too sharp for that. No, she had a much better, more natural idea…

And then after Flossy sadly died in her sleep tonight, she would admit, if it happened to be discovered, that Flossy offered to pay for her on the QT. She would confide to Flossy's children that she did not want anyone to know she could not afford it, and Flossy had been so generous, blah, blah, blah. With a torrent of tears, she would be completely believable. Flossy's children would feel so bereft, and have such compassion for her, they would honor their mother's wishes. And the torrent of tears would be real—she would truly miss Flossy. She even thought she loved her, but she loved herself more, so it could not be helped.

The ringing phone interrupted her reverie. Luckily, she had been sitting out the hand, as she never would have been able to concentrate on the cards. She picked up the phone, and it was the Cunard booking agent, just calling to confirm her reservation. Anticipating this possibility, she had given her home number instead of Flossy's when she booked. She was asked to repeat the credit card details. She had just said to herself she would remember those numbers whether they were written in her underwear or not, and so she repeated them quietly into the phone, although she was sure the girls were not listening.

But she was right in Flossy's sightline, and although Flossy could not hear the phone conversation over the ambient noise of the bidding, she *was* paying attention. She could clearly see what was being said. And Flossy too had a great memory for numbers, and she saw that her Amex card number was being recited into the phone. She was sure of what she had seen, but why?

And it came to her all in a rush. She and Frances had been right all along. The clues they had observed and Roberto had dismissed were all leading up to this moment...but, oh God—she would be the next victim. And she would be the victim tonight, she was sure of it. How had she been so dumb, so naïve? She wanted to jump up and throttle her friend, but instead she took some deep breaths to gain control. It would be a waste to have a heart attack now; she had to be ready to set the trap tonight. But it was hard to keep her heart from racing. She couldn't believe that no one else could hear her heart thumping right out of her chest.

At that moment, Flossy made a terrible play, and as the girls looked up from the table in wonder, they exclaimed, "Flossy, you look terrible. You are dead white!"

"That's an unfortunate expression," Flossy managed to joke. "I don't know, I just feel a bit faint. Perhaps I'll just sit this hand out, if you don't mind."

"Don't mind?" cried Faith. "Do you want me to drive you home?"

"Should we call Frances?" asked Babs.

"Let me get you a cold compress," said Mitzi as she headed for the kitchen.

"No, just let her put her head between her knees," suggested Dot.

"No, no, that will just make her dizzy. Give her some space and air. C'mon, Floss, come over to the sofa with me and I'll get you a glass of OJ. You may just need some sugar," said Gladys, who had quietly taken control. Usually the most ditzy of them all in ordinary situations, she was calm and collected.

And the orange juice seemed to work well. Flossy's color returned almost immediately, and she no longer looked so shaky. After sitting out for a few minutes, she rejoined the game and even won a few hands. Her friends were worried but thought it best to let her play.

What her friends did not know was that she was trembling inside, and her head was hammering. She covered it well because she was very determined…determined to make it through the night and determined to see justice done. She had discovered that one of her friends was a thief. She suspected that she was a murderer. Tonight she believed that Faith would show her true colors.

CHAPTER THIRTY-SEVEN

"Meessus Kane, I am here for you," said Frances, announcing herself as she came through the door. She twirled around the room to show the girls her elegant new coiffure, and she was accosted by five women.

"Frances, we have to tell you what happened." They all started talking at her at once.

"Ladies, ladies, wait, wait. Now don't you worry about your Flossy. This is not atypical if she didn't have enough to eat at lunch. What did you have for lunch, my Flossita?"

"I ordered a bacon cheeseburger, French fries, and a Diet Coke," Flossy replied.

"Yes, but she only *ate* the bacon," observed Gladys. "That's how I knew she must need some energy, and I ran to the refrigerator and poured her a glass of OJ, and she recovered almost immediately."

"Smart *muchacha*," acknowledged Frances, patting Gladys on the head. "And now I am going to get her home for a cocktail of some peanut butter and jelly and oxygen, followed by a nap. And she will be as good as new. And if you are not, I am afraid your date is off for tonight, my Flossy, as I am staying home!"

"Absolutely not—I won't hear of it! You are going to the ball tonight, my Cinderella, with Prince Roberto." Acting her old normal self, she stage-whispered to Faith like an ungovernable child, "And don't forget that chocolate cake!" But once Flossy left the girls and reached the car, she fell apart, hyperventilating and struggling for control.

"*Dios mio, que pasa, chica*?" questioned Frances as she soothed and comforted Flossy.

When she had had to, Flossy had brazened her way through the last hour, but once she was in the sympathetic arms of Frances, she could hold it in no longer. The tears began to flow, and only when the sobbing ended did she begin to relax. She leaned on Frances as they walked into her building, but she did not say a word. Frances knew Flossy would tell her what happened when she was ready, and in the meantime, she efficiently checked Flossy's vital signs and found them all to be within the normal range.

Flossy dug into the peanut butter and jelly because she knew she would need the energy, but she pushed away the oxygen and began to talk, calmly and in total control.

"Frances, we were right to be suspicious of Faith all along. I feel quite certain that she murdered Bunny, Paula, and Betty, and that tonight she intends to murder me. And it has all been for money; evidently she cannot afford this lifestyle. I am sure when Roberto checks her finances, and then he reviews our friends' credit card records, he will find proof and motive. This all became clear to me today when Cunard called to confirm her reservation and I *saw* her give *my* credit card number over the phone. She was speaking quietly enough not to be overheard while we were bidding at the bridge table, but I was looking right at her. Lip reading by habit, I could see her say, 'Yes, a veranda stateroom,' and then she reeled off my American Express number. 'Thank you for confirming,' she said. I almost fainted on the spot! Of course I won't have it. I want you to call Roberto right now, and this time he's going to listen to us. Together we are going to set the trap. If you and I had been more persistent in the past, some of my friends might still be alive." It was only with this last sentence that her voice began to waver. "So put those oxygen tubes in my nose, so I can take a power nap until Roberto arrives." She closed her eyes.

Frances called Roberto and told him it was an emergency and he had to come over immediately. Hearing the fear in her voice and assuming it had something to do with Flossy's health, he ran from the station house and dashed over, his siren blaring. For he too had come to love Frances's companion. He was puzzled when he arrived to find Flossy sleeping peacefully and Frances pacing the floor.

"My *chica*, what is all this about?" he asked, running his hand through his hair with just a slight air of impatience.

"Come with me." Leading him into Flossy's room, she whispered, "Just be patient and listen!"

Flossy, whose eyes were open, concurred. "Roberto, just as Frances told you, just be patient and listen."

"What is this, some kind of a setup? Frances whispers something and you pretend to have heard it? I *know* you can't hear, Mrs. Kane."

"Roberto, sweetheart, come sit down on the bed beside me. This is not a setup of any kind. This is a matter of life and death, and the death could be mine."

He started to protest, but she patted the bed and he sat as ordered.

"What you just witnessed, Roberto, quite coincidentally, so I do not have to prove it to you—although I will if you want—is that I may not always be able to hear what people are saying, but I can fake it if they are facing me because I can *see* what they are saying. So when you just walked into the room, I saw what Frances said to you.

"Now I'm going to tell you a story as it unfolded to me. I know when you hear it, more and more pieces will fall into place. Today at the bridge game, I saw my dear friend Faith give *my* Amex number over the phone to confirm her reservation for the Cunard cruise we are all planning in May. If you doubt my vision, or think I merely made a slight error, you can easily call Amex and find out if there is a reservation for Faith paid for by me. You will find it to be true."

"But how did she get your..."

"Patience—I am about to tell you more...a lot, lot more. Last week, she sat here with me while I was paying my bills. We got to talking about the price of the cruise, and I felt she wanted to say something to me but could not quite get it out. In fact, I asked her, and she said she was fine. I was explaining to her how to get two-for-one business-class plane tickets—you see she has not traveled that much to know—and I called Amex right then and there. We sat together on the bed while I stayed on hold, for, I don't know, five or six minutes, and I was holding my card right in my lap. Faith is good with numbers, and she could easily have memorized my card in that time. So, naïve me, the good friend, made the plane reservation for the two of us and told her she would not have to pay me until I got billed. And by the way, once the agent got on the phone with me, Faith excused herself to the bathroom. She could have easily written down the numbers."

"With what? On where? Did she take her purse with her to the bathroom or, better yet, a pad and pencil?"

"Don't condescend, Roberto. She could have easily taken a pen from my desk and written it on her bra or something. Go look in her underwear drawer!"

"Please, Flossy, I believe you can lip read and maybe even that she has stolen your credit card number, but why is this a matter of life and death?"

"Because I believe that all the little clues that Frances and I have observed lead up to my death. *Tonight*."

Frances saw that Roberto was about to lose his patience, but with a gentle hand she subtly restrained him. Flossy did not miss it.

"*Roberto,*" Flossy commanded in her most matriarchal voice. "Hear me out."

"Boy, you don't miss a thing, do you, Flossy."

"Put it this way, Roberto. A therapist once suggested to me I was very wary. I countered to him that I was not wary, just observant. He came to understand that it was true. You, as a professional whose powers of observation are essential, should recognize a fellow watcher. Now please, sit down and listen. I know I do not yet have proof of what I'm about to relate, but I will have proof tonight.

"The first of our friends to die was Bunny Boardman. Shortly before she died, we saw Faith at a department store—I can find you the date—and I *thought* I heard the salesgirl address her as Mrs. Boardman, not by her name, Mrs. Spector. She also scampered away like a frightened rabbit, as if she was hiding from us. The following week, Bunny's children hired a bookkeeper to manage her bills because she was so careless. And a week later, Bunny died of fish-oil poisoning at the movies eating popcorn with Faith. Pretty bizarre, but all quite coincidental, of course.

"Next thing we know Faith has befriended dear, sweet, muddled Paula. No one thought anything of it, but it seems to me it was the day Paula announced to all of us that she confused her pills. What an inspiration for someone who wants to shop with someone else's credit cards. You know Faith was at Paula's the day before she died. Then we ran into her shopping again, this time at the mall. She was laden with shopping bags, and although she explained that she was buying linens for her grandchildren who were coming down to visit, I could clearly see that the sheets were from Pratesi. One does not buy Pratesi sheets for kids. Just a petty lie and perhaps a mighty coincidence. But who left Paula a carrot cake the day she died? And who cast aspersions on our beloved Frances?

"And then there was Betty. If she had bought chips and returned them a half hour later, don't you think the cashier would have commented on her inebriated state when you interviewed him? I also wonder how come I saw Faith, conservative Faith, cashing in a fistful of chips at the end of the night? And I wonder if you interviewed him again, this time with pictures of Betty *and* Faith, you would find that the cashier could not tell them apart. And I wonder the same about that young croupier who was sneaking out of the bathroom. Betty was cockeyed drunk—but drunk enough to fall overboard? Again, I grant you, this is all speculation and coincidence.

"But tonight, tonight, my dear ones, we are going to use *me* as the bait. If I am wrong, you can send me off to the loony bin, but if I am right…"

"Flossy, Flossy, if you are right, she will *kill* you tonight. No, no, no, I will not let this happen," cried Frances.

At this point it was Roberto who restrained Frances. "Wait a minute, let's hear the rest. Flossy is not going to die to prove that she is right. She has a plan. Am I right, Flossita?"

"Oh yes, I do."

CHAPTER THIRTY-EIGHT

A man was telling his neighbor in Miami, "I just bought a new hearing aid. It cost me four thousand dollars, but it was worth it. It is state of the art."

"Really," replied his friend. "What kind is it?"

"It's twelve thirty."

Faith was scrolling through her e-mails, hammering her fingers on her keyboard. She snorted a sardonic little laugh as she read the joke sent to her by her daughter. "That's my friend Flossy all right."

God, she hoped Flossy was just dehydrated or something, not sick enough for Frances to stay home. Tonight's opportunity might not come again. She had worked out the scenario so completely, so *flawlessly*, it would be a shame not to have the chance to carry out her plan. And if she was blocked by Frances, who always seemed to get in her way, what would she do? Flossy would get her American Express bill in the next ten days and see two charges for the cruise—she would have to call and cancel her reservation, get Flossy's Amex charge cancelled as well, and then make up some inane excuse about why she could not go. She gritted her teeth and banged harder. Her new self was not used to being frustrated. Besides, if the cruise payment had already been charged, Flossy would see the debit and credit on her bill. She guessed this could be chalked up to an Amex error, but, but, but…Flossy was deaf all right, but that did not make her inefficient. No question she would call Amex to sort out the confusion, and then find out the charge was the payment for *her*. Oh, no, no, no…

Flossy was going to have to die, or she, Faith Spector, would lose her integrity…rather ironic.

At that moment of introspection, the phone rang. Noting on her caller ID screen that it was Flossy calling, she feared their evening together was going to be called off. On the other hand, if Flossy were really, really ill—having a stroke or something—she might get away with murder without actually having to do it! As she picked up the phone, she could not decide what to wish for.

"Hey, Faith, it's me, Flossy."

"Well, of course I know that, honeybunch, just by looking at my caller ID! How *are* you? I've been so worried about you."

"I am fit as a fiddle. Oh well, as fit as I'll ever be, I guess. Frances was right, I just needed a little nourishment, and I am expecting you for dinner. I am about to make my famous tuna fish salad, just the way we both like it—two spoons of mayo to one spoon of fish. Why worry about cholesterol at our age?"

"Right-o, sweetheart, and I am contributing my diet chocolate cake, ha ha! Do you want me to bring some wine?"

"Nah, you know I'm not that interested, unless you have a split of champagne on ice."

"For you, my Flossy, anything. In fact, I do, and I'll bring two splits—one for each of us."

"Dee-licious. See you at seven?"

"Until then. Ummm, how late do you think Frances will be?"

"My guess is that she won't be back until very late, but you don't have to stay until she gets here. You know I go to bed by ten when I'm home, and I don't need a guard to watch me sleep, for God's sake."

"I'll stay to tuck you in, honeybunch, and then leave you. Don't worry about my hovering over you. I know how you feel about being independent. You know I understand."

At that, they hung up. And Faith *did* understand Flossy, and she cared for her, but not as much as she understood herself and needed to care for her own needs. She had special regrets over losing Flossy, but it couldn't be helped. How much longer did Flossy have anyway...a year or two? And how much longer did she, Faith, have? She was determined to spend her last years enjoying life—no more sacrificing for all of Irving's poor patients, no more scrimping to get the kids through college and give *them* everything they ever wanted, no more caring for her aging parents, no more trying to be nice, no more boring, boring life. If she got *one* year, just 365 glorious fun and adventure-filled days, she would die happily. Two years, and she would be even happier...

Getting ready to go over to Flossy's, she reviewed her plan. Flossy had played right into her hands—wasn't it funny how these things happened—by asking for champagne. She had presumed Flossy would drink nothing but Diet Coke, and she planned to drop some sleeping pill powder into her glass when she served her. All that wasted time, tasting Diet Coke with Ambien to figure out how much to use before it tasted funny. Actually, it blended right into the fizzy chemicals of Diet Coke, as many as six pills worth of powder before it became noticeable. She would bring the powdered Ambien anyway—laced into the champagne it would work even better. She doubted it would change the taste much, and Flossy would become very, very tired indeed. Then when Flossy got into bed, she would wait around for a while until she fell into a deep sleep. After that, a pillow over her head with just a little bit of pressure and a loosening of the tube that led from the oxygen tank to Flossy's nostrils, wearing her handy rubber gloves, of course, and Flossy would sleep forever. Even if she woke up as she was being covered by the pillow, it would be so quick and painless it would not be cruel. She would rinse the dishes and tiptoe out without anyone knowing, ever, what really happened.

She knew that Frances often checked and cleaned the filter on the oxygen tank and changed the tubes for cleanliness. This time, it would look as if she had not quite reconnected everything correctly. That alone would not have been fatal, but Flossy had often told them that her pulmonologist *insisted* that she needed auxiliary oxygen every night in order to breathe, most especially when she was prone. She had survived the lung disease she had contracted the year before, but her lungs were irreparably damaged. She had surprised all her doctors by throwing away the portable oxygen tank they thought she would need to use every day for the rest of her life, but she conceded to using oxygen at night. Flossy's illness was never pinpointed, and her recovery was considered a miracle. No one would be suspicious or surprised if she quietly stopped breathing in her sleep, and coincidence of coincidences, especially after her "episode" at the game this afternoon.

It was all playing right into her little plot. No one would be blamed, except possibly Frances, for being careless. Flossy's children would be unlikely to ask for an autopsy, but even if they did, she knew Flossy had Ambien in her medicine chest. She had seen it when she went in the bathroom to write the Amex number on her panties. She would be sure to empty the bottle. Frances should *not* have left it there where Flossy could get hold of pills whenever she wanted them, and no one would question that Flossy had trouble sleeping after her "episode." She, Faith, would swear Flossy was asleep before she left. How would she have known that Flossy was swallowing down Ambien? And it could have been after she left, after all…

Yes, it was pretty airtight. Like all her victims, Flossy would seem to die from natural causes. How clever she was to figure out what they would *likely* die from and then just give them a little nudge. But she was anxious to get it over with. Her adrenalin was pumping, and she allowed herself a congratulatory little smile.

CHAPTER THIRTY-NINE

None of them were sure what *would* happen, but Flossy had pretty well convinced Frances and Roberto that whatever it was, it was going to be tonight.

Roberto argued for Flossy to cancel the date. Reluctant to place Flossy in danger, he would have preferred to incriminate Faith through financial records. But he admitted that even if he could prove that Faith stole credit card data, this alone could not convict her of murder. So he efficiently arranged for Frances and himself to be allowed access to Flossy's terraces through her neighbors' apartments. The terraces wrapped around the entire building with louvered walls demarcating each apartment's area—they were opaque enough to afford privacy, but they still allowed the sea breeze to waft through. A space of less than two feet separated the walls from the railings—not much room, but just enough to squeeze around in a hurry. He arranged for backup in the halls and for sharpshooters, with telescopic lenses on their rifles, to be posted on the terraces of the building directly across from Flossy's. As soon as one of his men saw *anything* suspicious, they would alert him so he and Frances could dash around the terrace dividers and be at her side in less than ten seconds. He would be on the terrace closest to the kitchen, as Faith would have plenty of opportunity to doctor Flossy's meal, and as soon as she did, he would leap through the terrace door.

He placed Frances on the terrace adjacent to Flossy's bedroom, should Faith get up to any malfeasance there. He instructed Flossy to pick up the phone if it rang, as he might have to give her spur-of-the-moment instructions. He knew this would not be unnatural, as everyone knew that Flossy was incapable of letting the phone ring without answering it, even if the caller was ID-ed as a polltaker or insurance salesman. He made Flossy swear she would keep her curtains open. He blocked all the locks on the terrace sliding doors, so even if Faith or Flossy closed them, he could open them from the outside. He continually reviewed every contingency. Only the bathrooms would be out of view, and he developed scenario after scenario of Flossy falling and smashing her head on the marble floor or, even worse, Faith tripping her, or...he didn't know what, but Faith was clever and imaginative. How could he get into the head of an eighty-three-year-old woman who murdered her friends for their money? He paced and paced, assuring himself he was doing the right thing.

Frances, always so calm in the face of the health emergencies she had weathered throughout her years as an aide, was beside herself. She could not stop imagining all the things that could go wrong with this plot and was already blaming herself for Flossy being hurt, or worse. But no matter how much she implored, Flossy would not be budged.

And Flossy was wide-awake, calm and determined. She was angry—furious, in fact—that her *friend*, in fact her favorite friend, had murdered and gotten away with it. She would not let her anger get in the way of seeing justice done, and on the plus side, her anger was giving her the energy she needed to set the trap. She had acted in amateur productions when she was young and had been quite good, even if she said so herself. This would be the hardest acting job of her short-lived career, but at least she had some experience. She would just have to put herself into the character of…well, herself—caring, funny, outspoken, and just a bit tired, of course. It would make sense after her little "episode" in the afternoon that she would be tired, and frankly she did not know how long her energy would hold out. She would go to bed very early and get the show on the road, as they said in the theater trade.

"So, my cohorts, are you ready to set me up as the poor innocent victim?" she asked mischievously.

"Oh, Flossita, I am so nervous about this. I would prescribe myself some Valium, but I have to be ready to pounce on that terrible woman, before she does anything to you," replied Frances.

"No, you don't, *chica mia*," admonished Roberto. "Let *me* do the pouncing, as you call it. I am only letting you stay to be an extra set of eyes, and because I can't think of what else to do with you," he teased. "Remember, this is the woman who threw Betty overboard—she is a power to contend with, I think."

"She would never have gotten Betty overboard if, one, Betty was not terribly drunk, and, two, if there had not been a storm that caused the boat to lurch. As I review these murders, I think killing Betty like that was spontaneous—Faith could not have predicted those conditions. I think the opportunity to steal money from Betty presented itself to her, and she grabbed it. She probably would have figured out a less violent way to murder Betty, but Betty must have caught her in the act…they fought, maybe even physically, and Betty went over the railing," Flossy surmised as she recreated the scene in her mind. "But the other two murders were well thought out, like mine has been, so I don't think she'll attack me in that way. Hence, I will be watching for every subtle move, don't worry. I'll even wear my glasses, okay, Frances?"

"Oh, Flossy, I know I am always bothering you to wear your glasses, but if you wear your reading glasses and she puts something in your drink a few feet away, you won't see it, and if you wear your distance glasses and she does it at the table, you won't see that either. *Ai, muchacha*…I *told* you to get bifocals! I actually think, although I can't believe I am saying this, that you should not wear your glasses, because you want it to seem as if everything is normal, and Faith knows you only wear your glasses when you absolutely have to."

Roberto further explained, "The riflemen stationed across the way will see everything for you and will alert me if they see anything suspicious. Meanwhile, if you feel at all uncomfortable for *any* reason, you must call out loud and clear. Do you remember what you are supposed to say?"

"Roberto, you have told me forty-five times what I'm to say. Do you think I could remember all the bridge hands of a game if I couldn't remember three words? I am not that nervous, really. I am determined to do this right."

Roberto raised his eyebrows and did not even need to say, "Well?"

"Okay, okay." Flossy staggered around the kitchen and feigned losing her balance as she cried out, "*I feel faint*!"

"Okay, enough with the drama. You have it, and you *are* a wonderful actress. Just don't ham it up too much. Feeling faint would be quite natural after your 'episode' this afternoon…so do *not* hesitate, do you understand me? This is the law speaking, Senora Kane."

"Yes, sir, Detective Gonzales. I don't want to get arrested for disobedience or, even worse, maybe…get murdered!"

"Not a funny joke!" Holding back her tears, Frances enfolded Flossy in her arms and held her as if she would never let her go. Regaining control, she went off to powder her nose and fix her hair one more time, even though she was really going no farther than the terrace next door.

The doorbell rang. Flossy took a long, deep breath, counted to ten, and answered it.

Faith told Roberto and Frances what a beautiful couple they made, and both Flossy and Faith fussed over them, taking their picture with Roberto's camera, fixing Frances's hair, and telling her to be good, but not *too* good. They told Roberto he would be the envy of his fellow policemen and ushered them out the door.

"Let's sit on the terrace, shall we?" suggested Faith.

"Of course. We should go out before it rains. It looks pretty ominous over the ocean, so let's go out for a drink and come in for dinner."

"Sounds perfect," said Faith as she scooped up the tray Flossy had laid out with two champagne flutes and a bowl of mixed nuts.

With her back to Flossy, Faith poured the champagne and proposed a toast. "To cruising the Mediterranean!"

As Flossy was about to toast back and drink her champagne, the phone rang. "Hold on a sec, Faith, I'll see who that is." Carrying her champagne with her, she sidled through the glass doors into her bedroom and picked up the phone.

"Not sure, Flossy, but don't take a chance. Pour out the champagne into the glass I left under the sink in your bathroom and refill with the champagne I left there. It may be a bit on the warm side, but suffer through it. Go now."

"Floss, where are you?" called Faith.

"Just running in for a pee before I come back out, sweetheart. I'll be there in a sec." Flossy did as Roberto had instructed, but did not tell him she had already taken a sip. *Oh well*, she thought, *what can one sip do*?

Flossy returned to the terrace, and then she and Faith watched the cloud formations gathering over the Atlantic. They talked about everything and nothing, but mostly about how beautiful it would be to spend two weeks on the sea. Flossy nursed her champagne while Faith drank another glass, leaning against the railing.

"Floss, you have *got* to look at this cloud formation," said Faith, leaning over the railing.

"Faith, you know I'm anxious about heights. I know it's illogical because I spend so much time on my terrace, five stories up, but I do love it out here. I relish the view from my chaise, but I can't lean over like that. As a matter of fact, it makes me queasy to see you do it. Come away from there!"

"Don't be silly. This is a strong railing…if you peek around the corner, it is really gorgeous. Come here, I'll hold you."

Flossy inched toward Faith and wondered if this would be Faith's ploy, but she doubted it—much too violent to drop her from five stories up, and what could she say had happened? But Flossy was frightened anyway because she really did get queasy about being on the edge of high places.

Meanwhile, Roberto on one side and Frances on the other were peering through the louvers, ready to rush if they saw any signs of a tussle. Their hearts were in their mouths, but Flossy quickly moved away from the edge as the first drops of rain began to fall.

"By the way, when you went inside, I thought I heard someone on the terrace next door," said Faith. "I thought you said your neighbors had already all gone north."

"I think they have," improvised Flossy, "but it could be their kids or friends, I guess, but most likely it is their revolting cat they leave here when they are gone. The super comes up and feeds her every day. Yuck! I normally hate cats, but I abhor this one. She is so arrogant! She comes through the space between the wall and the railing and prances around *my* terrace as if she owns it. I even find her sitting on my chaise, all curled up and comfy. Scat! I yell at the odious little beast."

As they laughed together about the imperious cat, she responded, as if on cue, with a loud meow. Clearly the cat was still there, as was Roberto, skulking in the shadows.

The rain started to pour on them, so they hustled inside, closing the sliding doors behind them. Faith started to close the curtains as well, but Flossy stopped her. "I never close my curtains, Faith. Leave them."

"You don't…I mean, people can see in from across the way."

"Puh-leez, Faithie, what are they going to see? First of all, they can *barely* see in, and even if they could see me *bare*, I doubt if the idea would cause them to get out their binoculars!"

They laughed at the idea of the old lady flasher as they ate their dinner, and Faith poured Flossy another glass of champagne.

CHAPTER FORTY

"Unfortunately, sometimes people don't hear you until you scream."
— Stephanie Powers, actor

Was it the laced champagne? Was it the strain of the day? Flossy was getting exhausted. How difficult it was to keep up the light banter and at the same time watch every move and anticipate. Anticipate what? As she sat talking with Faith, she worried she had made a huge mistake. Was she all wrong? She knew she wasn't, but how could Faith seem so natural? How could she be hiding her real self so effortlessly? Hopefully she too seemed natural, but the pressure was building. As she massaged her temples, Faith asked, "Floss, are you okay?"

"Of course I am. I must have a headache from all the tension this afternoon. Champagne usually cures it for me, but maybe I just need some chocolate cake to go with it." Flossy tried to be funny and stared wolfishly at the cake.

"Well, drink your champagne first while you finish your tuna salad. A second glass won't hurt you."

As Flossy was about to bring the champagne to her lips, she thought of Roberto's warning about the first glass that was bubbling under her bathroom sink and changed her mind. She had seen Faith pour the champagne into both of their glasses, but was it from the same split? Now she couldn't remember. Well, clumsiness would be the best policy, so as she lifted the glass again, she got up to get more mayonnaise on the counter and caught her toe (rather convincingly, she thought) on the edge of her chair and, in regaining her balance, dropped the champagne flute on the tile floor.

"Oh, what a klutz I am," she exclaimed as she bent down to pick up the shards of glass and this time almost fell for real on the wet floor.

"You sit right back down, and I will clean up," instructed Faith. "The champagne is no big deal, but your champagne flute looked like Lalique. Was it?"

"It was, and an antique as well. Our children bought us two for an anniversary, but it's just a *thing*. It can be replaced," sighed Flossy, thinking it was a small sacrifice for her *life*.

As Faith bent over the floor to clean up, she thought how cavalier Flossy had been about breaking a valuable antique and envied her for having so much that she didn't care. Had *she* owned Lalique antique crystal she would've been a lot more careful. And the champagne she had so carefully doctored for Flossy was oozing all over the floor. She hoped Flossy had ingested enough with the first glass to get sufficiently woozy. Her behavior—the headache, the unsteadiness—seemed adequate proof that it was already working.

Meanwhile, while Faith cleaned up, Flossy caught a glimpse of Roberto, peering around the wall into her kitchen. He had obviously been alarmed by the splintering of the glass, but Flossy waved him away, and he disappeared, just as Faith stood up.

"Okay, clean as can be. Now I've worked up an appetite for chocolate cake. How about you?"

Flossy didn't know how she was going to avoid eating it, even if she saw Faith serve her from one side and serve herself from the other, but thankfully she did not need to worry.

"You know, when I am alone, I do something so naughty," said Faith. "I would murder my kids for it."

Despite the unfortunate choice of vocabulary, Flossy could not help laughing as Faith took a huge fingerful of icing and sucked it into her mouth. Flossy did the same, and like kids waiting to be caught, they took bigger and bigger scoops, smearing the chocolate all over their cheeks and giggling. They eventually dug directly into the cake with their forks, doing away with the niceties of manners they so carefully cultivated in their children.

"Well, aren't we genteel?"

"The aristocratic ladies of Palm Beach!"

"La-di-dah!"

"And so lovely to meet you too, daaahh-ling!"

They burst into laughter once more, and this time Flossy held her stomach and said, "I have to stop or I am going to be sick, or fall asleep and never wake up!"

How prescient, thought Faith as she laughed with Flossy. Together they cleaned up, and Floss said, "Faithie, it's been great, but I *must* go to bed before I fall asleep on my feet."

"No problem, sweetie. You go ahead and get washed and undressed, and I'll come tuck you in."

And what else? thought Flossy, but she smiled and trudged off to her bedroom. Suddenly no longer tired, she felt a rush of energy, knowing that whatever was going to happen would play out in the next few minutes. She was frightened too, but felt protected, having seen Roberto right outside. So she put on her nightgown, brushed her teeth, and climbed up on her bed. She was fiddling with her oxygen tubes as Faith came in.

"Do you know what to do with that?" she asked, "or does Frances have to do it for you?"

"Don't be silly. Of course I do. This big box of a machine with its tubes that sits beside my bed looks intimidating, but it's easy to work, even for the technologically challenged. It's already set on the amount of oxygen I am supposed to get. So, *tah-dah*! I just flip the switch that says *on*, unravel the tube, put these little pieces in my nose, and I'm off to dreamland while my lungs replenish."

"Well then, I'll just stay a few minutes and dry the dishes and make sure you are safely asleep before I let myself out."

"Oh, sweetie, you don't have to stay, really."

"No, Flossy, I really want to—honestly, it's fine."

"Faith, you are a good friend." And for a second, Flossy almost believed it. She put her head down on her pillow, closed her eyes, and waited.

Faith did go to the kitchen. She dried the dishes and put them all away. As Roberto watched her he saw nothing suspicious in her actions, except that she washed out the champagne bottles a bit too carefully, but he knew these old ladies were often crazy about cleanliness, even if they were only washing bottles to recycle. What if she just let herself out and went home? What a fool he would feel. On the other hand, he would be sure that Flossy was safe. He did not see Faith pocket a small serrated paring knife as she headed for the bedroom to check on Flossy.

Faith tiptoed in, and sure enough, Flossy was breathing steadily and easily and seemed very much asleep. Wearing her rubber gloves, she snuck into the bathroom and emptied six Ambien from the bottle into the toilet. Flossy would never have taken that many, but she had to make sure that the bottle, which was once pretty full, was now obviously almost empty.

She was ready for the finale. Back in the bedroom, she bent over the oxygen machine and loosened the tube connection, using the knife—a last-minute brilliant idea—to scrape the metal and rubber connectors as if they had been worn, or run over by the vacuum cleaner. Out of her pocket, she pulled some lint she had gathered from her clothes dryer and rubbed it all over the filter. For a last little touch, she carved a few tiny slits in the tube. Now anyone investigating would blame Frances for not making sure all the equipment was in good condition. And she had one last thing to do. She had no idea that Flossy was watching through her eyelashes. She sidled over to the bed, and ever so gently, she lifted one of the pillows.

Flossy still had no proof of anything, although she feared what was coming. If she screamed now, Faith could say she was merely straightening the pillows and had been checking the oxygen machine. So Flossy tried to keep breathing normally and lay still as Faith lowered the pillow slowly, ever so slowly, over Flossy's head and held it there.

Now what? thought Flossy. *I can hardly yell 'I feel faint' from underneath a pillow, and yet in fact I do feel faint!* She felt a heaviness in her chest as she lay there, knowing the oxygen was not coming through the tubes. The pillow was pressing harder and harder against her face. She couldn't have yelled if she wanted to. Why didn't they think of this? Gasping for air, she thought, *My last request in life is going to be 'I need my Frances, where is...'*

And at that moment, with the shriek of a banshee, Frances came bounding through the terrace doors and leapt upon Faith. "You horrid little witch, get off my Flossita!" she cried. As she used all her strength to pull Faith away, they both fell onto the floor where they grappled like two spitting cats. As they rolled over each other, Frances pulled off her shoe and began beating Faith with its stiletto heel. Faith clawed at Frances and crawled away. Lunging after her, Frances pulled Faith to the ground once more. But just as Frances was getting the upper hand, Faith used all her strength to roll out from under Frances, pulled out her little knife, and scratched it across Frances's cheek. Although Frances was much stronger than Faith, she was shocked by the pain of the cut and momentarily lost her focus.

As Faith stood up, raising the knife as if to strike again, Flossy improvised a garrote. Kneeling on her bed behind Faith, who was staring down at Frances, she looped the circular part of her oxygen tubes that were meant for her nose around Faith's neck and pulled tight. Faith dropped the knife as she choked and lost control, while Frances wound the rest of the twelve-foot tube around and around her. Tightly bound in rubber tubing, Faith stood motionless.

Finally Roberto arrived via the living room with five heavily armed men backing him up. But the perpetrator was already in custody. He didn't know whether to laugh or cry.

"And where were you, Detective Gonzales?" demanded Frances, still breathing hard.

"I heard the scream and tried to get in through the kitchen, but Faith had closed the sliding door. With all the rain, I kept slipping and could not wrench it open, so I had to grope my way over to the living room door. I finally forced it open. I rushed here to the bedroom. My guys were coming in the front door. They heard the scream as well. Of course it was not Flossy, but you, my pet.

"Oh my God, you are bleeding!" Roberto, who had seen plenty of gory wounds in his day, who had not blinked at cadavers pulled out of Lake Worth, turned pale. He could not bear to see Frances hurt. Rushing to her, he tried to stanch the blood now flowing from her cheek with a handkerchief that did little good.

Flossy took over. She shouted at the policemen who were surrounding Faith.

"You two stay here with this despicable woman.

"You go to the kitchen for some ice.

"You go to my bathroom for some alcohol.

"You, don't just stand there! Go to the dining room and pour this girl a shot of scotch—a big one."

As they scurried to obey, Flossy turned her attention to Faith. "Faith, I just don't understand. *Why...why?*"

"You wouldn't understand," whispered Faith. "*You* wouldn't know what it is like to want all your life and not get, to watch all your friends take for granted what you struggle for. You just don't know."

"No, you poor, pathetic Faith, I don't. We all struggle for something. You were just too selfish and self-obsessed to see all the things you did not struggle for: your health, a wonderful, loving husband, children who care about you, friends who adore you. You just couldn't see it, could you? I am angry at you, Faith. I'm angry at you for taking what was left of the lives of our friends. But mostly I feel sorry for you…very, very sorry."

"You are too generous, Flossy Kane," pronounced Frances, loving her all the more for it. And looking up at Roberto, who would not let go of her, she asked, "Will you believe us next time we are suspicious?"

"Ahh, *chica*…I will believe anything you tell me."

"Will you still love me, even with a scar on my cheek?"

"I will love you all the more for the scar on your cheek."

And Flossy smiled at them. She felt very, very tired for real now and hustled everyone out of her bedroom, but not before Frances fixed her oxygen machine, cleaned the filter, changed the tubes, fluffed the pillows, and kissed her goodnight. She wanted to be sure Flossy would wake up in the morning.

"You saved my life, Frances, my love."

"You are the heroine, Flossita."

CHAPTER FORTY-ONE

"The boys are playing in their weekly poker game when suddenly Louie slumps over and dies on the spot. The men are horrified, not only that their friend of fifty years has died, but that now one of them has to tell his wife, Muriel.

"'Don't worry, boys,' says Herman, 'I'll take care of it.'

"The boys are all grateful to their friend Herman, as they are all a little afraid of Muriel. So Herman goes to her house and rings the bell.

"'Yes,' says Muriel.

"'Muriel, I have to tell you some news you may not like. Louie just lost a thousand dollars at the poker game and he is afraid to come home.'

"'Well, you can tell him for me, he can drop dead!'

"'No problem,' says Herman."

Gladys told the joke in memory of Betty. It was her favorite joke, and they all used to laugh, but none of them was really feeling silly. "C'mon, girls, life goes on."

"Oh, that's comforting," replied Dottie.

"Oh, Dot, Gladys was just trying to cheer us up," said Mitzi as she eyed a man she did not recognize walking through the club dining room.

"Well, at least some things never change," sighed Babs, watching Mitzi.

"Girls, girls, we just have each other now. Only five of us left… we have to make the most of the time we have left," chastised Flossy.

"Floss, I can't believe you are acting so *normal. I* would have been traumatized," fretted Gladys.

"Well, I do feel a little shaky from time to time when I remember what happened, but it's almost like a dream."

"Is it true that Faith tried to sedate you before she tried to smother you?"

"Yes, she dosed my champagne with super-strength Ambien, but I never drank it. I hid it under my bathroom vanity so it could be tested later. She was so clever. She knew I had Ambien in my bathroom, and she emptied a bunch of pills from the bottle the night she was with me, so if they ever did an autopsy, it would point to my taking my own drugs. And of course she counted on my lungs being the ultimate cause of death. Poor, poor, sick Faith. I bet she gets committed rather than jailed, but whichever it is, she will no longer be a danger to anyone.

"And despite the occasional shakes when I recall what happened, I feel strong and proud of myself, because in some way I have avenged the deaths of our friends. I have never done anything as important in my whole life…but of course, I can't bring them back."

"We girls of a certain age, we old bats—we're a dying breed, and there seemed to be a safety in our numbers, but now we're so few," lamented Dottie.

"Now we're so few, what?" asked Babs. "Do we go crazy, like girls gone wild or something? I for one know I can't go on the cruise we planned; it just has too many bad memories associated with it. And don't look at me that way, Mitzi. I'm not counting my pennies, I just want to make sure I'm happily spending them."

"Now we're so few, we should stick together as we always have, not let Faith do any more damage than she already has, and we should try to appreciate the good things we still have. Does that sound too Pollyanna?" asked Flossy.

"No, of course you are right, Floss, but I can't decide if I am tougher than I used to be or more vulnerable. What do you think?" asked Gladys.

"You know, I think we are both."

"True, true," they all agreed.

Sy came over to their table as they finished their lunch, hugged all five of them, and scooped Dottie up. "This old girl of mine—what am I going to do with you?"

"Take me to a ball where I will wear a gorgeous new dress and feathers in my hair," teased Dottie.

"Consider it done," said Sy as they walked out together, their heads leaning toward each other.

"You know, I think it was Shere Hite who said sex should be called something else and should include everything from kissing to sitting close together. I want *their* kind of sex," sighed Gladys.

"Well, go introduce yourself to that new man standing at the bar," instructed Mitzi.

"But I thought you had your eye on him," said Gladys.

"Of course I do. It's my nature, I can't help it, but I have a second date with a nice guy from North Palm Beach tonight who has invited me out on his *yacht*, so I am bequeathing this one to you. Can you believe he has a hundred-foot yacht?"

"I believe the yacht, but please don't say bequeath…we've had enough bequeathing these last few months. But, I mean, like, uh, what should I say to him?"

"Sweetheart, you just walk up to him and take a handful of peanuts from that bowl on the bar, and you tell him they are the *best* in all Palm Beach, and you just can't resist them. Would he like to try one? And then you offer it to him—just pop it in his mouth and smile," said Mitzi, giving Gladys a quick tutorial. "Here, spray yourself with some of this."

Gladys put on some lipstick, licked her lips, fluffed her hair, sprayed on the Chanel No. 5, took a deep breath, and headed for the bar. She was shortly in animated conversation.

"So, Babs, if we don't go on the cruise, what are you going to do?" asked Mitzi.

"Well, in fact, I may go on a different cruise," Babs replied bashfully.

"*Ohhh*, we get it," said Mitzi and Flossy in unison. "It's your fella."

"Well, I e-mailed him about what happened with Faith and all, and he got right back to me—not a postcard this time—he actually called. He invited me to join him on a ship this summer that cruises around the Scandinavian countries. Do you think I should say yes?"

"Of course we do. Would you seriously mind if we came too? No chaperoning, we promise."

"I would love that, I think I really would. It would make me less nervous. Will you come?"

"Well, let's just see what happens with my yachtsman," said Mitzi tentatively.

As Babs blew air kisses and was about to leave, Frances came into the club dining room to pick up Flossy. She still had a small bandage on her cheek, but she was full of beans. "So, girls, what are you planning now?"

"Well, they might join me on a cruise to Scandinavia this summer, right?" said Babs.

"Now you listen to Frances, Flossy Kane. You can't go on a cruise with your girlfriends and desert your faithful Frances. I thought we were planning to go to Paris together! You better build up your energy, *chica*, because even if you go on the cruise, we are going to *Paree* in September." And she began to croon, "September in Paris, chestnuts in blossom..."

"Frances, the song is 'April in Paris,' but September will be even more beautiful. Maybe you and I can join Babs on the cruise and *then* go on to Paris. What do you think? Will Roberto let you out of his sight for that long?"

Frances rolled her eyes. "Don't you worry about him, Flossita. He will let me go, but only if you are my *duenna*."

Flossy and Frances walked out together, arms entwined, planning their trip to Paris.

At that moment Mitzi's cell phone rang, and after a few minutes of "Of course I understand, of course I can understand that if your *niece* is coming to visit, we can postpone. Yes, thanks, I know you'll call me when you can." She hung up. Disconsolate, she looked up to see Gladys returning to the table.

"What's wrong, Mitzi? You look so downhearted."

"Oh, you know—the usual. My yachtsman's so-called *niece* is coming to visit, so my date has been postponed, but I have a feeling it's not going to happen any time soon. Oh well, new pastures await. What happened with you and the guy at the bar?"

"Oh well, the usual. He liked the peanuts all right, but he's waiting for his girlfriend...humph."

And they both cried at once, "Babs, Flossy, Frances—wait for us!"

ACKNOWLEDGMENTS

Thank you to my friends, who laugh at my jokes and keep sending me new ones; to my children and grandchildren, who listen to my stories and give me ideas for upcoming sequels; to Brian Hotchkiss, who adapted his considerable editing skills to the mystery genre; to Camilla Trinchieri, whose writing I admire, for her encouragement and advice; to Rona Roberts, my companion on many visits to Palm Beach, who knew my characters and helped me bring them alive on paper; and to Joy Fox, who let me freely adapt the poem she wrote about her father.

And most of all, thank you is not nearly enough to my husband, Allen, whose love has enabled my life.

ABOUT THE AUTHOR

Photograph by Felice Yager, 2012

Jane Grossman divides her time between homes in Boston and Aspen. Before moving to Massachusetts, she and her husband lived in New York City, where she cofounded and ran the famous Traveller's Bookstore in Rockefeller Center. She has a B.A. from Barnard College and is the coauthor of *Boston Foot Notes: A Walking Guide*.

Made in the USA
Lexington, KY
17 February 2013